MYSTERY ON THE

FOURTEENTH FLOOR

Dorothy Martin

MOOD'
CHIC

Printed in the United States of America

1

Vickie spread a thick layer of strawberry jam on a third piece of toast and chewed the sweet crispness as she stared out across the courtyard at an apartment building identical to her own. The window shades in that one apartment two floors up were in the same straight line as they had been every one of the other twenty-four mornings she had looked at them. She glanced down into the courtyard and then slowly raised her eyes, looking at the ivy-covered bricks of the opposite building.

Every morning since moving to the apartment in the middle of June she had eaten breakfast in the plant-filled end of the big, high-ceilinged dining room. By the time she got up, Mother and Dad and Francine had already gone to their exciting jobs. She had nothing to do but stare at the rows of windows in the apartments facing her. People must live behind those blank windows, but she had never seen anyone.

A lot of the windows had those fancy white shades. But this apartment was different because its shades were always in the same even line. She wondered how the people who lived there all knew exactly how far to raise the shades.

Vickie's gaze wandered again and she sighed. Another day and not one single exciting thing to do. It had been that way ever since they had moved to the city three and a half weeks ago. She fished the last marshmallow from the bottom of her cup, rolled its sogginess into her mouth, and morosely stared out the window.

Then she stopped, swallowing the marshmallow in surprise. One of the white shades hung in a crooked line and was lower than the others. She counted up from the ground. *It would be the thirteenth—no—fourteenth floor,* she thought.

Dad had explained once why some large office and apartment buildings did not have a floor thirteen. He had agreed that it was silly to be superstitious about a number.

She looked back at the window again and blinked. Was she seeing things? She had glanced away only for a minute, and in that instant the window shade line had again become even and unbroken across all eight windows. Someone over there certainly was fussy about the way things looked.

Vickie grinned to herself. Whoever it was, he would go crazy in her room. One of the neat things about Vickie's family was the way each member was willing to let everyone else live the way he wanted—within limits, of course. To allow each family member freedom was one reason they had moved into the middle of the city, away from the tree-lined streets and neatly manicured lawns that had been home for her all through grade school. Right after last Christmas it had been decided that her mother's artistic talents needed more opportunities than a house in the suburbs could give them.

"I've been a good neighbor long enough," she

had insisted to her husband and Francine and Vickie. "For years I've welcomed new people to the neighborhood with chocolate cakes and home baked bread. I've run my share of car pools to school and swimming and tennis lessons, and served my years on PTA boards. Now I want to do *my* thing. And that means being in the city where I can have my own studio and become a serious artist. I want recognition!"

She had brought the last word out with a laugh, but Vickie knew that under the laughter she was serious.

Her father had agreed and they had hunted for an apartment large enough for her mother to be able to turn one room into a studio and still leave three bedrooms, a den, and a spacious living and dining room. Even then it would be smaller than the big house Vickie had grown up in, with its five bedrooms, family room, and big sun porch overlooking a wide lawn.

Vickie knew her mother loved being in the city, with art galleries and museums available at the other end of a bus line, and with taxis responding to her wave.

Dad was happy about the move too. "I've always wanted to be close enough to the office so that I could walk," he said.

Vickie noticed, though, that he usually flagged a taxi, too. But at least he did not have to fight traffic to get to the office.

"One good thing about a law office is that it doesn't usually open before the birds are up," he said. "So I can eat breakfast with you on school days."

Vickie abruptly turned her mind from the dreaded thought of school and back to her family.

Francine was crazy about the city, too. She had graduated from college a year ago with a degree in broadcasting and right away had got a job with a TV station. She told everyone she was a TV reporter, which she was—once in a while. At first Francine mostly did just routine, behind-the-scenes things. But this summer she was going out on more stories. Vickie remembered how her mother, afraid Francine might get hurt, had stewed around the first time she had gone out to cover a big fire. Another time she had been in a mob of people at the airport when the president came through. All they got to see of her then was her hand clutching a mike, which she tried to shove close enough to the president to hear what he was saying to a reporter from another channel.

Francine loved the excitement of living in the city where she said "all the action is."

It's funny though, Vickie thought. Generally the exciting news took place somewhere across the world and sometimes even in the suburb where we used to live. Usually the news was just miners striking or Congressmen talking about taxes and inflation.

Right now, though, every news report blared details of the kidnapping of a six-year-old boy. It had happened two days ago, and the kidnappers had not sent any ransom note yet.

Vickie sighed. Everyone else in the family lived such exciting lives. Dad would never admit that he was a famous lawyer, but he must be. People were always calling him for an appointment, and they paid a lot of money for his advice.

Mother was getting to be famous, too, and already had set up a showing of her paintings for next week.

Francine had made it on television, even if sometimes Vickie saw only her fingers clutching a mike. She even looked like a famous person. She wore super clothes. When she tossed back her long blond hair in that eager way she had, her steady boyfriend, Pete, looked at her in that special way that told he was really gone on her. And Francine was really nice, too, never telling Vickie to get lost, the way the sisters of some of Vickie's friends did.

"And then there's *me*."

She said the words out loud. It was bad enough to be twelve, which was such a dumb age. But to be twelve and not have talent for *anything* was awful. She was not one bit artistic, even though everyone expected her to be. Teachers always said, "Why, Vickie, dear. Naturally I thought *you* could draw a house. You have such a talented mother."

And she couldn't talk like her father. She remembered going once to hear him argue a case. She had watched a couple of the women jurors wipe away tears when Dad described the rats and cockroaches in the unheated house that the defendant had grown up in. But when *she* had to give just a simple old book report in front of the class, her mind went blank and she could not remember even the title of the book.

Worst of all, she was not tall and leggy and blond and self-confident like Francine was. And she never would be.

She was just pudgy Vickie, who was dumb in math, had to wear glasses and braces, and in just six weeks faced the horrible prospect of going to a new school in which she would not know anybody. If only there were some way to turn herself into a smart, beautiful, talented *somebody,* life would be so much better. Then she would not mind starting a new school, even without a single friend to stick with. If only she looked different, if she were a whiz at tennis or something, everyone would want to be her friend.

Vickie peeled and ate a banana and drank a can of pop while she thought about her problem. If she really put her mind to it, she should be able to figure out some way to get—what was the word Dad used?—notoriety. She liked the sound of it, especially when Dad said it. He really knew how to use words so that people remembered them.

Vickie propped her elbows on the table, her hands cupping her cheeks. What made people famous anyway? Take Dad for instance. With him it had to be his brains and his ability to make people go along with whatever he said. He could use mile-long words, and just the way he said them made people understand their meaning, even if they had never heard the words before. And when he stood by the railing of the jury box and smiled at the twelve people sitting there, they just automatically smiled back at him. Then they leaned forward to listen because each juror thought Dad was talking only to him. Dad had what people called charisma. So with him it was both brains and personality.

"Which I don't have," Vickie reminded herself.

Mother? She was so self-confident about her art. Personally, Vickie could not see that her paintings were that good. She had looked at them right side up and sideways and upside down, and they looked just the same from any angle. They had been simply big swabs of blues, reds, purples, and oranges all run together. But she had learned not to make comments about them.

Once when she was in nursery school she had watched her mother work on a big canvas and had said, "I didn't know big people did finger painting." And she could still remember her mother's hurt reaction at her father's shout of laughter.

But people came to her mother's showings and said things such as, "Fascinating the way she has captured the spirit behind the meaning"; and, "Can't you just *feel* what she is trying to say?" Then they actually paid hundreds of dollars for the paint blobs. Didn't that prove the paintings were good? And that Mother was talented?

Of course with Francine it was her looks. Her tall, model-thin figure and long blond hair caught everyone's eye. Vickie had noticed that when other women reporters stood on a windy street corner giving a news report, their hair looked stringy and tangled. But Francine's hair just tumbled around her high-cheekboned face in deep, ruffled waves and looked as though she had combed it that way.

Her teeth were white and straight and did not have the wires that made Vickie look as though she were an advertisement for a hardware store. And then there was her voice—low, throaty, and happy sounding, which made people want to listen to her. So she had looks, brains, talent, and charisma.

"And then there's me!" Vickie said the words out loud again, letting disgust at herself spill out. She pulled the spoon out of the squat jam jar and licked it clean.

"I'm not artistic, and I can't talk well, and I'm not pretty. So how can I be somebody in a family where everyone else already is someone?"

She stared out the window again and looked up at the white shades in the apartment window. Then she leaned forward and squinted. Something white was plastered against the window glass. It looked like a piece of paper with black marks or lines or something on it. She got up and pressed her face against the window and put her hands on either side of her face to shield her eyes. But the sun's glare reflected on the white paper and she could not tell if the lines were words.

Vickie frowned. She would be able to see them with Dad's binoculars. But she was not supposed to use them that way. In the park watching birds it was OK, but Dad had warned her against using them at other times.

"It's an invasion of privacy to use binoculars to look at people in their own homes. In fact, it is spying, and we have laws against that sort of thing."

Vickie peered again at the intriguing white paper in the opposite window. Because this was Monday, Mother was still home, working in her studio. Maybe she could figure out if the marks were words.

10

Vickie jumped up, lugged her dishes into the kitchen, and then went along the hall to the studio. Nuts! The door was closed, and her mother's splashy sign reading, NO ADMITTANCE EXCEPT IN CASE OF FIRE OR STARVATION, was on the door.

The clock chimed in the living room and Vickie counted. Ten o'clock. That meant Mother would not be out for at least an hour. If she were going really well on the painting she might work longer. And if she were just standing there scowling at her work it might be even longer, because she always hated to stop when she got to a place where she couldn't see her way out.

Vickie turned and walked back to the dining room again and stared across at the other apartment. She couldn't see anybody at the window and she wondered if someone over there could see her. Feeling silly, she gave a half wave and then waited. No one waved back.

She looked down onto the courtyard that separated the two buildings and watched the water spraying from the fountain in the middle of a circle of green grass. The fountain was especially pretty at night, when colored lights played back and forth across it and reflected shimmering sprays of blue and green. Concrete-enclosed circles of grass intersected the tree-lined walks that connected the two sections of the apartment complex. A high brick wall with an ornate white iron fence surrounded the two buildings and set the apartments off from the main sidewalk. Then a wide parkway of grass and thick, trimmed shrubs separated the buildings from the street and made the traffic constantly speeding by only a muffled hum instead of a disturbing roar.

When they had first talked about moving, her father had asked Francine if she wanted her own apartment.

"Why? With you I have security and with my job I have independence, so I have the best of both worlds. If I lived alone, I wouldn't have anyone to share my day with. And if I had a roommate, I'd have to give her equal talking time. Besides, I'm kind of fond of you guys."

Francine had found this apartment and had argued for it passionately.

"If we're going to leave our beautiful home with all its memories, then I think we should get an apartment that is elegant and old-worldish," she insisted. "And I've found exactly the right one."

"Old-worldish?" her father had echoed, his eyebrows shooting up to almost touch the streaks of silver that tipped his black hair. "With two—no, three—liberated women in the house, the idea is incongruous."

He was always tossing out words that Vickie didn't know. But this one she had figured out without any trouble. She had just finished reading a book about the immigrants who had come to America from Europe years ago. It had a lot of pictures of women coming down gangplanks from boats. Most of them had scarves on their heads and wore long skirts. They all carried bundles of things, and most of them had a baby in their arms and other children clinging to their skirts. The captions under the pictures talked about people coming from the "old world."

Now if *that* was old-worldish, then Dad was right. Francine and Mother in their mod clothes and knee-high, thin leather boots were incongruous.

Anyway Francine had flipped when she saw this building with fancy carvings around all the windows and a beautiful fountain in a courtyard surrounded by magnolia and redbud trees. She had begged her parents to look at it, at least. When they did, Mother went wild over it, too.

And it did not take much to convince Dad when he saw its convenience to the office. Vickie remembered her first ride in the wood-panelled, carpeted elevator with a mirrored ceiling. At first she thought even the elevator was old-worldish until she found it went up so fast that she was there before her stomach was ready. It moved so silently that she had to watch the floor numbers slide by to know the elevator was moving.

Vickie stood by the window and thought back to all the excitement of the packing and moving. She had been swept up into the adventure of change. When Betty Lou and Sandy came in to see the apartment, they were really impressed.

"Wow! Look how different things look from up here," Betty Lou exclaimed.

"And look at the neat place to skateboard," Sandy pointed out. "You can really go in circles around all those walks down there."

The move and settling in had offset the loneliness—until now. Betty Lou and Sandy had stayed overnight a couple of times the first week. But now Betty Lou's family was in London where her father went on business, Sandy was visiting cousins in California, and everybody else was in camp. If she had known how dull life here would be, she would have gone to camp again this summer, too.

This business about the other apartment window was the first excitement to come her way. She scowled at the thought. She was really low if a crooked window shade was exciting to her.

Vickie leaned against the window frame and drummed her fingers on the marble window sill. She tried to line up where the windows would be if they were without the white shades to make them easily seen, and figured they were straight up from the largest magnolia tree.

"Maybe I can see better from a different angle down below," she muttered.

She got the silver chain and key that her mother had personalized for her with her initials, *VM,* done in elaborate curlicues, stuck a candy bar in her shorts pocket, and let herself out of the apartment door. Only an occasional, muffled sound of a vacuum cleaner, stereo, or TV from other apartments let her know she was not alone in the building.

She walked the length of the carpeted hall and rang for the elevator. In a moment the doors slid open with a soft sighing sound and Vickie plummeted to the ground floor. She felt her stomach had not really been adjusted to the ride before it was over. Her rope sandals made a plopping sound on the marble-tiled floor of the lobby as she walked past the doorman. Mac stood behind his desk with its battery of phones and buttons that connected with each apartment. He shook his head at her, his wide grin showing white teeth.

"You'll get a tan just stepping outside in this heat. Like mine," he added.

Vickie smiled back. "I won't stay out long if it's that hot because my candy bar will melt."

She pushed through the revolving doors and felt what he meant. She squinted into the blinding glare and wished she had worn dark glasses as she walked around the courtyard, stopping to look up at the windows. But she found she could see even less on the ground than she had at her own window. When she tilted her head back to look up into the blinding sun, her neck muscles ached.

She finally gave up and went back upstairs. As she closed the apartment door and heard the automatic lock click behind her, her mother called, "Vickie?"

Mrs. Montgomery came from her bedroom, adjusting an earring and looking cool and elegant in her lemon-colored sleeveless dress.

"Honey, I hope you don't mind my dashing off before lunch. I got an unexpected luncheon appointment that could be a very important contact. I had fixed us some tuna salad early this morning and there's lots of fruit in the refrigerator. And you'll probably want to swim this afternoon. The temperature is frightful, as you probably discovered when you were meandering around down there in the courtyard going blind staring up at the sun. Whatever were you doing?"

"Oh, nothing."

She had planned to show her mother the sign in the window to see if she could figure it out. But she changed her mind. There was probably nothing to the sign anyway.

Mrs. Montgomery leaned toward the mirror to put on lipstick and then turned and said earnestly, "Honey, I'm sorry you are alone so much. We had no idea when we moved here that your friends would all be away. I wish we had insisted that you go to camp for the summer."

"Don't worry. I'll call someone and talk a while. I think Marge is home."

Her mother grabbed her purse, slipped a handful of sketches in the slim, wide leather case she invariably carried, and reached to give Vickie a hug.

"Back about three, I think."

Vickie went to the window. The white paper was gone, the window shade line was even, and there was no sign of anyone in the other apartment. She waited until her mother came out of the building and until her light, quick steps took her across the courtyard to the white iron gate. Vickie saw her arm lift to hail a taxi, which swept her out of sight.

It was not really time for lunch, but there was nothing else to do. So she fixed herself two tuna sandwiches, sliced a tomato and sprinkled salt on it, and poured a glass of lemonade. She sat down at her favorite place at the glass-topped table at the far end of the dining room. Mother and Francine had turned that end of the room into a miniature garden with plants surrounding the table.

After waiting for her lunch to settle, she got into her swimsuit, took the elevator down to the recreation floor, and went out to the pool. It was crowded with young mothers, shiny with oil, sunning themselves while their children shrieked in the water.

Vickie looked around carefully as she had every other time she had come down to swim. Not once in the twenty-four days had she seen anyone her age. If any lived in the building, they must be away for the summer. None of the noisy kids running around was more than five years old.

Moving here had not changed life one bit for Mother or Dad or Francine. They had even more exciting things to do now than they had had before.

But she had lost everything. Her friends were too far away to be seen every day. She couldn't do any of the fun things she had been used to, such as riding bikes with Marge and Sandy, listening to records with Lynn, talking for hours about nothing with Betty Lou, skateboarding with everyone on the block. The whole summer was going to be like this, just blah. And then, when it ended, she faced the horrible prospect of going to a new school where she would not know anybody.

2

After dinner that evening Vickie wandered into the dark dining room and looked across at the other apartment building. Even though it was still somewhat light out, it was hard to spot the right windows when the row of shades did not show up clearly.

She jumped when her mother spoke suddenly behind her. "Why are you standing here all by yourself in the dark? I know we are supposed to conserve energy, but that doesn't mean you can't have a light when you need it."

She touched the switch so that the bright lights of the overhead chandelier blazed; then she adjusted the dimmer switch for a softer light and asked, "That better?"

Vickie looked around at her mother, saw the concern on her face, and knew her mother was worried that she was lonely. She *was* lonely, of course, but there was no point in making her mother feel bad.

So she gestured out the window. "Everything looks different at night, doesn't it? The lights stretching down the street look like rows of jewels."

"Yes. The city is beautiful with all the lights in the buildings reflecting the stars. The darkness covers the dirt and grime."

"Betty Lou was surprised to see the apartment

when she came to visit. She thought city apartments were little boxes, and everybody could see into other apartments when they opened the bathroom medicine cabinet—like on TV ads."

Her mother laughed and then sobered immediately. "We have to remember that we live in a beautiful part of the city and in a beautiful apartment. Not everyone is that fortunate. Many people live in areas where we wouldn't."

Vickie looked up at her mother in the semi-darkness of the room and heard the groping sound of her voice as she went on. "Dad and I hope you haven't found the move too difficult. I'm sure you will find life more exciting when school begins and you make new friends."

"Oh, sure." Vickie tried to make her voice sound nonchalant, unconcerned.

Her mother gave her a quick, reassuring hug, went back through the living room, and called over her shoulder, "There's a pretty good program on television you might want to see."

Vickie looked across at the dark windows of the building opposite her and started to turn away. Just as she did, a light flashed quickly on and off in the mysterious window. As she watched, it flashed three more times in rapid succession and then three more times.

Vickie looked around to be sure her mother had gone and then dashed across to the wall switch and turned the chandelier lights on bright and then quickly off, three times. She hurried back to the window in time to see the lights in the opposite apartment flash as they had before. Then, though she switched her light on and off

19

several more times and waited, the other window stubbornly remained dark.

She went to her bedroom and sat down at her desk. Did that light flashing so deliberately on and off mean something, or was it just that someone couldn't get a lamp to stay on? Could it have been a signal? She switched her desk lamp on and off, trying to imitate the way the other light had flashed.

"Now what?"

At the sound of her mother's amused voice coming from the doorway, Vickie looked around. "You seem to have an obsession about lights tonight."

Vickie said loftily, "I'm just doing an experiment," and thought, *How can you be a detective and unravel a mystery when you yourself get spied on all the time?*

A sudden thought hit her. *Maybe that was an SOS! How many flashes were there? Three? Four? There were spaces between them.*

She drew lines on a piece of paper, / / /; then another group, / / /; and another, / / /. That was the way the light had seemed to flash. Suddenly she realized that that was the way the lines on the paper in the window had seemed to look that morning.

The Girl Scout manual, which she had had the year she had been a Scout, had something in it about sending signals. She hunted for it along the shelf above her desk. Naturally it wasn't there. She wouldn't hang onto a book she hadn't used since fourth grade.

Dad would know what an SOS was like. She

jumped up and went along the wide hall to the den. He was in his big leather swivel chair, a pile of papers on his lap and a symphony playing on the stereo.

"Dad, how do you do an SOS signal?"

He looked up at her and closed the book he was holding, putting a finger between the pages to hold his place.

"An S is three dots and an O is three dashes or lines." He reached into his pocket for a pen and demonstrated on a piece of paper.

. . . — — — . . .

"But how do you tap it out?"

"Like this."

Vickie watched and listened as he tapped his fingers on the arm of the chair and said at the same time, "Dot-dot-dot, dash-dash-dash, dot-dot-dot."

Then he looked at her as she sat on the edge of the couch and watched. His eyebrows arched the way they always did when he was amused by something, and he asked, "Are you trying to send a call for help to someone?"

"No, just—curious."

She looked at him and wondered how much she could ask without getting his lawyer mind suspicious.

"Can you—not just you, I mean, but anyone— send that kind of signal in other ways? Using other things? Like—oh—I don't know. Flags or—or lights or—"

"Or bedsheets or smoke signals?" he finished, with laughter coloring his voice. "Yes, just so you

21

get the proper sequence and keep the right intervals between the signals. The dots would be shorter and the dashes longer. Like this." He tapped the rhythm again, more slowly.

But his eyes and voice were serious as he looked across at her. "Of course you understand an SOS is only used as a distress signal, a call for help. It doesn't have any other meaning—should not be used for any other purpose. It's a time-honored signal used by ships at sea. When they are in danger of going down, they send out an SOS for help, hoping other ships will hear and be close enough for rescue."

Vickie nodded, not wanting to explain her interest. She was saved from having to answer the clear question in her father's eyes by Mrs. Montgomery's excited dash into the den, her voice breathless.

"Quick, put on the TV. Francine is on in a special news report."

Vickie clicked on the TV and they watched the picture focus on a crowd of reporters clustered around a police official who was holding them back with a gesture.

"Look! I've told you all I can. We can't release all the information we have because we must think of the safety of the little boy. We don't want any news leak that might make the kidnappers do something drastic. As soon as we can give more details we will. Try to think first of the little kid's safety and not of getting a scoop on a story."

The reporters' voices broke into a babel of sound. Vickie got a glimpse of Francine, her arm stretching out and holding a mike to pick up all she could of the conversation. Her face was alive with excitement and her long blond hair spilled over her pale blue blouse.

"I wish she were not mixed up in that kind of news reporting," Mrs. Montgomery fussed.

"But it's so exciting." Vickie's voice showed her envy.

"It's also dangerous—going out on assignments about kidnappings and robberies—"

"Don't let your imagination get carried away, Louise," Mr. Montgomery interrupted. "Just standing in a group of reporters that size and talking to the police, Francine is a long way from danger. Ten months in a job barely qualifies her to go out on an assignment. She's lucky to get as many of these as she does. You know she could have been put into an office to file reports."

Vickie listened as her mother argued, "That's just my point. Why does she get sent out on assignments in the bitter cold or on these hot days? There must be jobs in the studio she could do."

Her husband laughed. "What's happened to your zest for equal rights? If men go out on dangerous assignments, as you call them, women reporters should carry their share. Isn't that what equal means?"

"Danger is something else," his wife argued stubbornly.

"You know Francine eats it up," he answered. Then he sighed. "I only hope I'm asleep before she gets in or she'll keep us up the rest of the night telling everything that happened before, during, and after the interview."

Then he sobered. "Maybe instead of worrying about Francine's safety, we should think about the little boy and his frantic parents. We got an anonymous call in the office today asking if we would handle the defense of the kidnappers if and when they are arrested. So obviously something is developing in the case. Whoever is involved is willing to pay a big sum for the defense. I'm against it, of course. I told Milligan I would have no part in it. How can you possibly defend kidnapping even under our system that says a person is innocent until proved guilty? Milligan claims that since everyone is entitled to a defense lawyer, our firm might as well get the money."

Vickie stood up. There was no use waiting to ask the other important fact she needed to know about SOS signals. How to send a signal back was the question she needed an answer for. Did a person send the same signal or a different one?

Just as she stepped into the hall, she heard her mother asking a low question, with a faintly amused sound in her voice.

"Carl, I'm curious. Is that a Bible on your desk? I didn't know we had one."

"We didn't. I bought one a week or so ago. I'm just curious, that's all, Louise. A new man in the firm, a nice young fellow, said one day when we were having lunch together that the trial of Christ was the most unfair trial in history. It was held in secret, the witnesses were paid to lie—that sort of thing. It intrigued me. He got my lawyer curiosity aroused to read the transcript of the trial. And of course the only place to get the transcript firsthand is in the Bible. So I bought one."

Vickie heard the laughter coloring her mother's voice as she answered, "Well, as long as that's all there is to it, I won't worry. I can understand intellectual curiosity. I just don't want you to become too involved in strange notions."

Then, before she could move away, her father's voice came again, a note in it she had not remembered ever hearing. His voice sounded unsure, searching.

"I've staked my life on the idea that a good lawyer hears both sides of a case before reaching a decision. I've never done that with Christianity. I wonder if I have cheated myself—"

Vickie heard her mother's urgent protest. "Carl! You're already perfect! What more do you need?"

The closeness of their voices made Vickie feel like an eavesdropper, so she went out to the kitchen, pulled open the refrigerator door, and stood frowning into it, hungry for something good.

There was lots of fruit, but also a piece of chocolate pie left from dinner, and she reached for the pie. Francine would not touch it when she came home even if she wanted it. One thing Francine really had was will power not to eat stuff that might make her gain weight. And there was no sense in sacrificing it for Pete. He always brought Francine home when she worked late and he never refused food. Francine could scramble him some eggs or grill him a ham and cheese sandwich.

She put the pie on a big enough plate so noth-

25

ing would spill. Mother was pretty lenient about not making a clean house more important than her family, but she did draw the line against chocolate stains on the pale blue carpet—especially if the stains were made by someone standing in the dark, looking out the window, and carelessly eating chocolate pie.

When she finished eating, she stared across at the windows in the other building where lights glowed softly behind closed drapes. Then, suddenly, something clicked. Francine, kidnappers, and unexpected signals from the window across the courtyard whirled together in her mind. As they whirled, all the pieces came together and made a picture that raised goose bumps of excitement along her arms.

The kidnapped boy was over in that apartment! She was sure of it. She remembered the scraps of information Francine had reported at her coffee and toast breakfast the day before, when news of the kidnapping had just broken.

- He had been visiting his grandparents who lived on the north side of the city.
- He apparently had gone willingly with the kidnappers, which might mean he knew and trusted them.
- His parents were very wealthy and could be expected to pay a big ransom.
- He was a smart little boy, not easily scared.

What better place for the kidnappers to hide him than in a fancy and respectable apartment building where no one would think to look for him? It always happened that way in books and on TV. The clues were always in plain sight but no one ever saw them until the great detective pointed them out.

Well, she was no great detective, but she could see a mystery when it took place right under her nose and was practically handed to her. Tomorrow she would go across to the other building and "case" the floor. When she was sure she had the right apartment, she would tap out a signal to let the little boy know she had got his message. Then she would call the police and lead them right to him.

Vickie's smile in the soft darkness was triumphant. Then she would be somebody, too, and maybe Francine would interview her on television.

3

Waking up and looking out the wide expanse of her bedroom windows, beyond the cars whizzing by below, and across to the lake shimmering in the sun was one thing about the apartment that Vickie still was not used to. The water probably would not sparkle in the cold of winter, but it certainly did today.

She sat up in bed in a pool of warm sunshine, her arms hugging her knees. Then she scrambled to the edge of the bed and stretched from under the blue ruffled canopy to pull the drapes open wider. Opening the drapes brought the reminder of the crooked window shade in the other apartment and the sheet of white paper plastered against the glass. The shade and the white paper might not mean anything, but the light flashing last night certainly had to be a signal for something. That something was a call for help. She was sure of it.

She jumped out of bed and went through the quiet apartment. The carpet was smooth velvet under her bare feet. Dad had already gone, of course. She knew that when she heard the clock strike nine. Francine had probably gone to work, too, in order not to miss any of the excitement in her job. She had come home last night after Vickie had been in bed. Vickie had heard Francine's voice spilling out all that had happened during the day, but she had been too far under to make herself get up to listen.

Since this was Tuesday, the silence in the house meant that Mother had gone, too. Sure enough, the note propped against the toaster said:

> You were dead to the world, so I didn't try to waken you. Have gone to the art museum and will have lunch there. Plan to be home by three-thirty. Have left some goodies in the refrigerator. Tomorrow let's plan to *do* something.

"Good," Vickie muttered the word out loud. "Now I won't have to sneak around to do my investigating."

The words made the whole thing sound important. She poured a glass of orange juice and padded over to the dining room window. The shades in the mysterious apartment were in the usual straight line. No note was plastered against the blank glass of the window. She counted up from the ground floor again to be sure she had the right apartment. Some time the kidnapped boy might have time only for a quick signal and she wanted to be able to spot it right away. Since so many windows had similar white shades, she studied the building and looked for some way to identify the apartment. It was the apartment with a row of scarlet geraniums set in brackets along the balcony railing. Other balconies had several kinds of flowers; this was the only one just with geraniums.

A thought caught her as she turned away to fix herself breakfast and she stopped, worried. Would

29

a six-year-old know about an SOS signal? She tried to remember herself at six. Had she known what an SOS was? Or how to send it? No. She was just now learning it.

But then of course she had never been kidnapped nor been in any kind of dangerous situation. She had never needed to send a signal of distress. A person in a tight spot probably could remember things and do things he never thought possible before. Dad had told about a woman who had singlehanded lifted a car off her child when he had been pinned under it in an accident. In cases like that, Dad said, a person somehow got superhuman strength. Knowing SOS signals was not exactly the same thing, but the idea was the same.

Anyway, she knew one thing for sure. *Somebody* over there was sending a call for help. And somehow she was going to answer it.

She hurried out to the kitchen, fixed a bowl of cereal, thickly spread two slices of toast with butter and jam, added a doughnut to the plate, and poured a tall glass of milk. She carried the food in to the glass-topped table and settled down into the best position for watching. She ate by feel, not wanting to take her eyes away from those windows.

But nothing happened. No signals of any kind appeared and the shades hung motionless. She felt disappointed, cheated of something that had promised excitement and challenge.

Then she reminded herself that the boy would have to be careful about the signals. He could only send them when no one was watching. Probably the kidnappers were with him now.

She thought back. When had she seen the first change in the window shade? It had been yesterday about this time because she had been eating breakfast. Nothing had been different at noon. Then the lights had flashed last night after dinner. Had the little boy been left alone those two times? Of course she had no proof those were signals, but she had to track them down to be sure. She could not call the police until she had definite information. The best way to get it was to go over to the other building and be on the scene of the crime. Maybe she could ask questions of the doorman in that building. If he was as nice as Mac, she might worm some information from him without giving away her reason for asking.

She carried her dishes to the kitchen, rinsed them, and stuck them into the dishwasher. She pulled on shorts and a shirt, ran a comb through her hair, and reached for the apartment key. When they had moved, she and Francine had been warned to be careful. Dad had bought each of them a small whistle and had put it on a silver chain. And he had given stern instructions about using it in an emergency.

He had said, "Francine, you especially must be careful. But you too, Vickie. Keep alert when you are out on the streets or even in the building. Don't automatically trust anyone."

Vickie had thought the warning overdone. So far she had not seen anyone who looked like a criminal. Then she was jolted by the reminder

31

that a real live crime was taking place right across from them. And it was up to her to stop it.

She started out the door and then stopped. Her head was cocked in thought and a frown lined her forehead. Should she wear a disguise? And if so, what?

She went back into her room and looked around. What did people wear when they did not want to be recognized? Just wearing different clothes would not be enough of a disguise. She would have to change her face and hair. But how?

She wheeled around and went across the room and through the connecting bathroom into Francine's room, pulled open the double closet doors, and looked up at the round, silver-colored boxes that lined the top shelf. Here was the answer to a hair disguise. Francine had gone through a wig craze for about a year. She had six boxes on the closet shelf, each one neatly labelled as to the style and color of wig.

Vickie got the small stepstool from the kitchen broom closet, climbed up to the boxes, and read the labels silently. She would not bother with the brown wig. It would be too ordinary, too much like her own hair.

She took the top off the box labelled "blond Afro wig" and carefully lifted out the wig. Francine had worn it only once and had not liked it. As soon as Vickie put it on she knew it was too big. She tried pushing it back but every time she moved her head the wig slid down past her eyebrows. She climbed down and looked at herself in the mirror, made a face, and took it off. If they were all that big she was sunk.

The black wig with the bangs was also too big. Then she tried on the red one and found it was smaller and fit more closely than the blond one. It must be one that Francine had bought when her own hair was shorter. Since she had let her hair grow out, the wigs had to be large enough for her to tuck her own hair under them. Of course now she was completely off the wig kick, thanks to Pete.

"I don't like false hoods," he had said once, teasingly. But Francine had taken him seriously and had quit wearing them. She was really gone on Pete.

Vickie put the boxes back and climbed down. She tried on the wig in front of the dressing table mirror. Wow! It really made her look different. It stuck up in a funny way, though, and needed brushing. She pulled open the drawer where she had seen Francine put her wig brush. She felt guilty doing it. Not borrowing another person's belongings without asking was one of her parents' strictest rules.

"But when you are a detective, you sometimes *have* to break rules," she argued back at herself, "especially when the detective work is helping to rescue a small, scared child."

When it was all over she would tell Francine about borrowing her stuff and she would understand.

But looking at herself in the mirror, she frowned at her reflection. With a wig like that making her look older, she needed something else—lipstick at least.

Now that she had borrowed the wig without asking, she might as well borrow whatever else she needed to make her disguise complete. She sat down on the round, blue-padded swivel chair in front of Francine's dressing table and looked at the jars and bottles of makeup. She sure had a lot. Of course, she knew how to use makeup so that even Pete thought all the color was her own. Boy, was he in for a surprise when they got married.

When a bunch of kids last year had started wearing eye makeup, Francine had said, "Don't get started wearing it too soon, Vickie. Your eyes are so pretty—big and round and yet sort of slanting, and such a beautiful brown—people always notice them, even behind your glasses. The natural look is the big thing now anyway, according to all the makeup experts. So if you don't need it, don't bother with it."

Vickie was glad for the advice, because the few times she had used eye coloring it took so much time to put it on right.

Now she decided to try the blue eyeshadow and some mascara. It was a cinch that she needed something to make her look older than twelve. The eyebrow stuff made her eyebrows look too wide, but at least they really showed up now. If someone tried to describe her later, about all he would remember would be her red hair and very black eyebrows.

When she tried to put on the mascara, she got too much on the brush. To steady her hand, she rested her elbow on top of the vanity. But even so, the mascara got on her cheeks under her lower lashes and smudged when she tried to wipe it off with a damp tissue.

When she finally stood back and surveyed herself, she scowled at her image. She really looked nutty now with all that fancy makeup and hair and just a pair of cutoffs and a tee shirt for clothes. What could she wear to match her looks? Francine's clothes were out because she was so much taller and thinner.

She looked at herself and tried to stop frowning, because it brought her eyebrows too close together. The eyebrow stuff made a straight black line across her forehead, from the outside edge of each eye, and made her look really strange. She rubbed at it, but only succeeded in making the skin look dirty.

"This is supposed to be a disguise, not a clown outfit," she muttered to herself.

Finally she changed into a dress and sandals. Maybe nobody would notice what she was wearing. People would be too busy looking at her hair and face.

Vickie was glad she was home alone as she let herself out the apartment. She could not have done all this if her mother were home, even if she seemed to be locked in her studio. Sometimes her mother got a guilty conscience about neglecting her, and came out to see if Vickie needed anything.

The hall outside the apartment was empty as she had expected it to be. She had never seen anyone from the other three apartments on their floor during the week. Saturdays and Sundays occasionally, but not on weekdays. The elevator was empty, too, and she was glad no one was on it to stare at her. As she dropped to the ground floor, she realized she had not planned what to say to the doorman if he did not recognize her and asked who she was and what she wanted. For that matter, what could she say to him if he *did* recognize her and asked the reason for the disguise.

Fortunately Mac was helping a little old lady find a coded apartment number on the directory board, so she breezed right past him. Naturally he did not check people who went out of the building. It was the people coming in that he had to be sure belonged.

That was going to be the problem in the other building. How was she going to get past the doorman to get up to the right floor? She stopped outside the revolving door, out of the lobby, and squinted up at the other building. How would a real detective figure out what to do? Maybe it was better to do nothing at all than to do the wrong thing.

"I wish I'd read more detective stories," she muttered out loud.

A woman coming out the revolving door behind her asked, "What did you say?"

"Uh—nothing." Vickie turned her head away from the startled expression on the woman's face. She had forgotten about all the makeup she was wearing. Getting anyone suspicious of her was the main thing to avoid.

She strolled along the tree-lined walks that intersected the apartment complex and stopped to watch the fountain spraying up water. Two little children were kneeling on the low wall and reaching their arms through the bars of the white iron fence, trying to touch the water drops. Vickie looked at them and wondered how old they were. She was tempted to ask them if they knew what an SOS was, but decided not to. Her face might scare them.

She walked out to the high brick wall, stood by the white gates, and looked up and down the street at the traffic whizzing by. A laundry delivery truck passed her and slowed to turn into the driveway that led to the basement entrance behind the building. She idly watched the truck inch its way along the narrow driveway.

An idea exploded. Of course! That was her answer. The delivery man had to open the basement door. She could get in when he did and take the elevator from the basement. That way she would not even have to see the doorman because the elevator would go right up to the floor she wanted. But she would have to hurry to get through the basement's outside entrance when the delivery man did, because she did not have a key for it.

Her sandals clip-clopped as she ran along the hot sidewalk and turned into the driveway. The truck driver was lifting piles of clean clothes from the back of the panel truck. He piled a stack of clothes over his arm, but the plastic-covered garments kept sliding from his grasp as he tried to hold them up from the dirty cement of the driveway. Several shirt boxes fell. When he stooped to get them, he dropped several of the plastic garment bags.

His face was red and sweaty as he muttered words under his breath.

"Want some help?"

"What do you think?" He growled over his shoulder without looking at her. Then he turned to face her and grunted, "Oh, sorry, kid."

He took a second look and grinned. "You can hold these bags for me, but just keep your face away from them, okay? If the lipstick and the rest of that goop rubs off on the plastic, some of these dames will insist they have to be done all over again. And for free. So you know who'll have to pay for it? It'll come out of my hide. Here. Grab these boxes while I get the door open."

"Do you have a key?" Vickie watched him fumble for his wallet.

"Are you kidding?" he snorted. "The management of these buildings don't give out keys. They don't trust nobody. We get issued these special cards that are harder to duplicate. They fit in this slot. Like this."

Vickie watched him insert a plastic, numbered card into a narrow opening high on the side of the door.

"See?" he said. "When the numbers register the right combination, the door automatically opens. They change the cards all the time to keep the security tight."

He looked at her over the top of the pile of garments he was holding. "You live here?"

She nodded. "Yeah. But in the other building."

Then she asked, "Where do you take all this stuff? Do you deliver to each apartment?"

"Are you kidding?" he asked again. "I'd spend all day running around and most people wouldn't be home. Nah. It all goes to a room across the hall over there." He nodded in toward the basement lobby. "Everybody who sends out laundry, gets a notice stuck in their mailbox when it comes back."

He looked at her skeptically. "You sure you live here?"

"Oh, yes," Vickie answered quickly. He could not doubt her now when she was so near to getting in. "We've only been here about a month, though, so I guess I've never noticed about the cleaning."

A buzzer sounded, and the lock was released. The laundry man pulled the handle and held the door open with one foot while he reached in to stack the shirt boxes on the floor. Then he backed in with the garment bags draped over his arm.

"Thanks for your help, kid."

"You're welcome."

Vickie started to follow him in, but he blocked her as his foot still guarded the door.

"Hey, sorry, kid. I can't let you in. The doorman's been reading the riot act to all us guys. Last month someone let in some kids and they fooled around in the elevators. Scared a couple of old ladies."

"But I live here."

"I know, I know. But that's what those kids said too."

"But I really do," Vickie protested. "Look."

She pulled the silver chain out from around her neck and showed him the key with the apartment number clearly stamped on it.

"Look, kid. *I* believe you. But I still can't let you in. Especially when you don't actually live in this building. Anyway, why do you have to come in the basement entrance? You can go around to the front and get the doorman to let you up if you're visiting someone here."

He looked at her then and laughed. "Oh! I get it. You don't want anyone to see you in that get-up. I don't blame you. What'd you do it for anyway? It's too early for Halloween. Or maybe you're going to a masquerade party. One thing's for sure, no one could forget you. See you, kid."

He gave her a cheerful grin and pulled the door tight.

Vickie turned and scuffed her way back along the driveway to the main sidewalk. Now how was she going to get into the building? If security was that strict, she would never get by the doorman without knowing the name of the people in that apartment. And there was absolutely no way of discovering their name.

The sun beat down on her head and her face felt sticky from the sun's glare on her makeup. She could feel the perspiration on her forehead trickling from under the wig, but she was afraid to wipe it away. The makeup would get more smudged than it had been to start with.

She clumped back along the sidewalk to the white iron gates. Then the significance of the laundry man's words hit her.

"Nobody could forget you," he had said.

But that was not what she wanted. She wanted to be able to slip in and out without being noticed. Her disguise should be the kind that was so plain that no one would look at her twice.

12—Mystery on the Fourteenth Floor

The answer was so simple that she felt stupid for not thinking of it in the first place. All she had to do was be herself. She would go home and wash all this stuff off her face and put on her usual shorts and shirt. But first she would stop at Mac's desk and get some advice from him about how to get into the other apartment. He was always so friendly when she went in and out of the building.

4

Vickie pushed through the revolving door into the lobby coolness, hoping no one else would be there. The laundry man's remark that she looked as though she were dressed for Halloween made her realize how silly she looked.

But she saw a group of women clustering around the doorman and asking directions. Vickie ducked her head and reached up to shield her face by pretending she was fixing the wig. She stood with her back to the women and looked at the plants in the circular greenhouse that filled the center of the lobby.

Finally, when the clicking high heels of the women had taken them across the mosaic, marble-tiled floor to the elevators, Vickie turned and walked slowly toward Mac. Her mind raced, trying to figure out what to ask him about the mysterious apartment.

Mac grinned at her. "I don't think I know you, Miss," he said in mock seriousness. "Are you sure you live here? We aren't letting circus people in today without proper identification."

Vickie forced herself to smile back. She had seen a distorted reflection of herself in the clear glass of the greenhouse and knew how wild her face looked. She was getting tired of being the butt of jokes. Then she had a sudden inspiration.

"I was going to play a trick on someone in the other building. There's someone over there I want to see. But I don't know the exact apartment number. What shall I do?"

"Well, the same thing everyone does here," he replied. "It's the same system. Find the name on the directory board and call the code number. If whoever it is is home and wants to see you, she'll tell you the apartment number and let you in."

Vickie thought quickly. What to do now? She couldn't say she did not know the name because that would be a dead giveaway that she knew nothing about the people at all. Inspiration came again.

"Well, yeah, but, you see, I really wanted to surprise this person. You know, not let 'em know I was there until I was—there." She let her voice dribble off and waited for his answer.

"Um—well—" He rubbed his chin as he frowned down at her. "Management is pretty strict about letting people in without being sure they belong. Things could happen, you know, if we were to let just anyone in. People could get robbed, and then we're the ones who would get the blame for not checking more carefully. Of course—you *do* belong here—"

He stopped and studied her, his frown deepening and his voice becoming stern as he demanded, "You planning to rob this person?"

His eyes smiled as he asked the question. Then he said, "OK, I guess I can help you. What floor do you want?"

Vickie thought quickly. If she had counted right it was the fourteenth. She had better sound positive and not raise any more questions in his mind. So she said firmly, "Fourteen."

He considered her again, his doubtful frown back. "Are you sure this person, your friend, wouldn't mind if you appeared unannounced at the door?"

She nodded. "I'm sure this person would be very glad to see me." She hoped he would not notice that she had not said it was a friend.

"Would you if you were in her place?"

"Oh, yes!" She answered so emphatically that he laughed.

"OK. I guess I can trust you. You go on across and I'll call over to Charlie and describe you." He stopped and chuckled. "Not that he could miss you."

"Yeah, I do look pretty awful," she agreed. "Maybe I'd better go up and get cleaned up first. I guess it's not a good idea to let this person see me like this. He—she might get scared and slam the door in my face."

She slid through the lobby door he unlocked for her and was thankful he had not noticed the slip of her tongue. Her mind was so full of thoughts about the little boy that she just naturally had said, "he." She rang for the elevator and hoped she could get on it and get upstairs before anyone else came along. The fewer people who saw her now, the better she would feel.

When the elevator doors quietly slid open with the usual little oiled sigh, she met the startled gaze of two elderly ladies as they stepped out. Vickie looked around at them as they stared back over their shoulders at her. She heard the beginning of the comment, "What is *wrong* with that child's

44

face—" before the doors closed and the elevator zoomed her up.

She turned the key in the lock and opened the door of her apartment cautiously. What if Mother had changed her mind and had come home early? What excuse could she give for her appearance? She did not want to tell of her suspicions just yet. She stepped inside, closed the door silently, and stood listening. It was quiet. The tick-tock of the grandfather clock in the wide sun-lit hall sounded loud in the empty silence.

She rushed into the bathroom, ran hot water in the washbowl, bent over it, and vigorously scrubbed her face with a washcloth.

When she raised up and looked at herself in the mirror, she exclaimed in panic, "Oh, no! It's not coming off!"

What did Francine use to take off makeup? She dashed into Francine's room and looked along the glass shelf of the dressing table at all the pretty jars of glosses and creams. She kept on talking out loud.

"I should have watched her put the stuff on *and* take it off. It never looks like a mess when she wears it."

Finally she found a jar of cream that took off most of the makeup. The eyebrow stuff was the most stubborn and even repeated applications of the cream, and then of vaseline, left her eyebrows still looking darker than normal. She frowned at her image. She would have to do some more work on the eyebrows before the rest of the family came home. But finally it was her own face, instead of

45

a clown's, that looked back at her from the mirror.

When she was clean and back in shorts and shirt she could feel the hollow place in her stomach. All the running around and planning had made her hungry. It was not time for lunch, but maybe a banana and a handful of peanut butter cookies would help her figure out what to do next.

She walked over and stood by the dining room window while she munched the cookies. The next thing to know was which apartment to go to on the fourteenth floor since she did not have a name to ask for. But another thought crowded in to worry her. Maybe it was an empty apartment the kidnappers were using just to stash the little boy in while they waited to collect the ransom.

She shook her head at that. No. The doorman kept too close a guard on who went in and out. But that thought ran a cold prickle of fear along her arms. That would mean the kidnappers must be perfectly respectable-looking people whom no one would think would do something so awful as to kidnap a six-year-old child.

Suddenly other complications crowded her mind that she had not thought of before and she tried to think of answers. How had they got the little boy past the doorman on duty to begin with? Why had he not hollered for help? Maybe he had and people thought he was just being a bratty kid.

Why didn't he stand at the apartment door over there now and yell? Well, maybe they kept him gagged. No, that could not be true. His hands must be untied because he was making those signals, and so he could take out a gag, too.

"What if I'm imagining the whole thing?"

She asked the question out loud and the thought was almost a disappointment because of her eagerness for this to be a mystery that she could solve. Maybe she had just so much longed for something interesting to happen that she had imagined the whole thing—the crooked window shade, the lights flashing. The piece of paper in the window could have meant something else—or nothing. After all, she had not seen any words on it. Maybe it was not even intended for her to see.

But as she stared across at the windows, doubts crowding her mind, the proof came. A piece of white paper appeared in the window again. This time three dark black letters showed distinctly, with spaces between them.

S O S

What other proof than that did she need? Determination stiffened her. She whirled, dashed to her room for paper, scrawled a huge O K on it, hurried back, and held it against the window glass, waiting for an answer. None came. The SOS sign remained flat against the glass.

She counted up from the ground again—yes, it was the fourteenth floor. Then she counted the number of windows from the edge of the building. If that one had the same layout as their building, it was a corner apartment with windows on the other side also. But now what number would it be?

She stood tapping her fingers on the marble sill, wondering how to find out. Then she remembered the building chart that Dad had before they moved, which showed the layout of all the apartments and their numbers. Had he kept it?

If so, where would it be? Probably in the drawer he called his important miscellaneous file and which her mother called his squirrel file.

Vickie went to his oversized desk in the den, found the chart in the drawer, and studied it. Yes, she was right. It would be a corner apartment for sure, and the number would be 1492B. That should be easy to remember. Knowing that much for sure should get her past the doorman with no hassle from him.

She went back to the dining room window and peered out intently. The sign with the black SOS was gone, but as she watched, another one appeared. It had a word on it this time, a short word, but she could not tell what it was. A thought came slowly: binoculars would show the word clearly. She argued with herself over it. It would not hurt to use them just this once. That would not be spying on anyone. She turned and walked, her feet dragging, back to the den.

Dad kept the binoculars in the bottom drawer of his big desk. She had seen him put them there a couple of Saturdays ago when they had come back from birdwatching in the park. His big soft leather chair swallowed her as she sat down in it. After a moment, she leaned to pull open the drawer. The binoculars were there in the brown leather case.

When she lifted the case out, she saw a sheaf of paper-clipped pages. Out of curiosity, and without thinking, she picked them up. Her father's careful printing, done so neatly and swiftly with his left hand, filled the lined pages. Vickie glanced down the first page. He had printed:

Fact	Scripture
He was born miraculously	Matthew 1, 2; Luke 1
He claimed to be God	John 10
He did miracles	
healing (lame, blind)	John 9 and others
made food	John 6
raised dead people	John 11 and others
He knew people's thoughts	Mark 2
He rose from the dead	Matthew 28; Luke 24

Caught by the evidence of the careful study her father was doing, Vickie stopped in her rush to get the binoculars. She sat holding the pages, looking at the first fact he had listed, and thinking back to the manger scene she had had one year when she was little. Some friends had given it to her and said it belonged at every Christmas celebration. It had been the only religious thing about their Christmas. That year their tree had sparkled with glittering, fragile ornaments. Another year Mother had filled the tree with puffy, red velvet bows. Last year the tree had been all pink. The manger scene had been the only religious thing they had ever had. Until Dad bought his Bible.

She clipped the rest of the unread pages together and put them back into the drawer. It had taken only a couple of minutes to look at them, but she felt as though she had spanned centuries in ideas. Guilt weighed down on her. By breaking family rules and borrowing without permission, she had also snooped into her father's personal life, invaded his privacy. The words on those pages showed her the conflict going on inside him.

But she argued herself out of the guilty feeling about using the binoculars. This was a special emergency. She was not spying just to spy. It could mean life or death for a helpless little child. The thought was scary, but it stiffened her determination. Dad would understand when she told him—when it was all over and she had saved the little boy. She snatched up the binoculars before she could change her mind and hurried back to the window.

Though she had used the binoculars lots of times before and knew how to focus them, her fingers shook with nervousness and it took a couple of minutes to adjust the glasses. Finally the letters on the white paper leaped out at her.

H E L P

Vickie caught her breath. That settled it. The sign had definitely been put there for her to see. It had appeared just after she got to the window. The little boy had seen her and had his message ready.

Did that mean the kidnappers had left him alone for a little while? They must have or he would not be able to signal for help.

Again questions beat at her. If he was alone, why didn't he open the window and yell for help? It must be he was tied up except for his hands. Then why didn't he use the phone? He surely knew his own number or could dial the operator and get help. The answer to that must be that there was no phone in the apartment. For some reason he needed help from an outside source. And he was making her that source.

The thing to do now was call the police. She hurried to the kitchen phone and looked at the list of emergency numbers that her mother kept on a shelf by the phone. She picked up the receiver and then stopped. What would she say? They would certainly ask her for proof. Could she give a crooked window shade and a scrawled "Help" sign in the window as proof?

She hung up the receiver and turned slowly. Her mind was a jumble of confusion. Dad always said, "Get evidence. Be sure you have your facts straight." It could be she was trying to make a mystery out of something that was not a mystery. The signs could be done by someone just trying to be funny.

She went back and stared across at the window again. It was empty. Maybe—maybe if she went over, she could simply knock on the door and see what would happen.

She wheeled around before she could change her mind, put the binoculars back on the sheaf of papers, took her key, and let herself out the door, deciding not to leave a note for her mother. How could she explain when she herself did not know what the situation was? Anyway, she would be back long before Mother got home.

On the way to the elevator, she detoured to check the number of the apartment on their floor that corresponded to the apartment number across the courtyard. It was 1192B on this floor. Two floors up would be 1392B, only they would call it 1492B.

Now, if she acted as though she knew what she were doing and whipped off the apartment number when the doorman asked whom she wanted, he might let her up without asking questions.

Francine was always saying, "You have to *act* self-confident if you want other people to think of you that way. People judge you by your estimate of yourself."

"Now's my chance to see if that really works," Vickie told herself as the elevator doors opened on the ground floor. She took a deep breath, straightened her shoulders, and walked past the desk in the lobby with a casual wave at Mac.

"I know the apartment number." She tossed the words over her shoulder.

"OK. I'll run interference and call over so Charlie will let you up."

The sun's glaring heat felt good this time because she felt shivery with an excitement mixed with fear.

She had not let herself think of the other big problem facing her. So far her plans had been just to get past the doorman and up to the fourteenth floor. But what would she do after she got there? How would she get into the apartment if the little boy was tied so he could not let her in? And he *had* to be tied, because if he were not, he could get out by himself and would not need help.

Her heart beat hard at another, even worse, thought. What would she do if the kidnappers came back and caught her? They certainly would not let her off scot free.

She stopped by the fountain to think through the questions. Should she let someone know what

52

she was doing, where she was going? She looked around uncertainly. If she waited until Mother or Dad came home, it might be too late. That HELP had looked too urgent.

Of course she could tell Mac or Charlie her suspicions—

But this is my *mystery*! She had not really said the words out loud, but they sounded loud in her mind. There was more to it than that, of course. She still had the sneaking fear that she was wrong, that there was no mystery at all.

Well, she had come this far. She would just have to take the chance that she was doing the right thing. She hurried across the courtyard and into the other building. One part of her mind noticed that it was exactly like their lobby—the same mosaic, marble-tiled floor with peacocks spreading their beautiful tails in each corner of the floor; and a circular greenhouse, filled with tropical plants and a rock garden, in the center.

Her breath eased out in a sigh of relief when Charlie lifted his hand in a wave and walked over to unlock the lobby door.

"You must be the gal Mac said to watch for."

He did not ask after all which apartment she wanted. If he had, she might have had problems getting through. If he knew the tenants the way Mac did in their building, he would know there was no girl her age in that apartment. Then he might not have let her up.

She pushed the button for the elevator and waited. Now that she was so near the really dangerous part, she felt cold with goosebumps of nervousness on her arms. A man got on the ele-

vator just as she did and pushed the ivory knob
for the sixth floor. She waited until he got off
before she pushed fourteen. The rest of the family had warned her about being in an elevator
alone with someone she did not know, but she had
listened impatiently. Now the thought of riding
an elevator with kidnappers, who might look like
normal people, made her shiver as she remembered the advice.

When the elevator stopped at floor fourteen and
the doors yawned silently, Vickie held them open
with one hand while she put her head out and
looked around. No one was in sight and no sound
came from any apartment. It seemed safe. She
got off, the doors slid shut, and the elevator's soft
sigh indicated it had started back down. Lights
burned the length of the hall which stretched
straight ahead and on either side. Down at the
end of the hall sunlight streamed in the window.
1492B would be somewhere down that hall.

As she stood motionless, a telephone rang
shrilly over and over in a nearby apartment. It
stopped and then almost immediately began again.
When it stopped, the dense quiet made her even
more nervous. What if she needed help and absolutely no one was home to hear her cries?

"Maybe I won't need anyone." She said the
words into the silence, licking her dry lips, trying
to reassure herself.

She walked along the hall and turned the corner
toward 1492B, the sound of her steps lost in the
carpet. She could not help glancing nervously
back over her shoulder. The silence made her feel
as though unseen eyes were watching her. How

could a building that was so full of people in a city that was itself bursting with people be so empty and quiet?

When she got to the door with the gold-lettered number 1492B she listened. No sound came from inside. She held her breath and put her ear against the door. Was the little boy just on the other side, waiting for her help, unable to call out?

After a moment she tapped lightly on the wood door. There was no answer. She knocked again, louder. As she did, a phone rang sharply from the next apartment, scaring her and keeping her from hearing any response from the other side of the door.

The telephone rang insistently twelve times before it finally stopped. When it did, Vickie pulled out the paper she had stuck into her shorts pocket. She had copied the SOS signal and tapped it lightly on the silent door, saying the words to herself.

dot-dot-dot, dash-dash-dash, dot-dot- dot

Faintly but very distinctly, the signal came back to her from behind the closed door.

dot-dot-dot, dash-dash-dash, dot-dot- dot

5

The sound dropped into the silence of the hall so faintly that Vickie wondered if she had really heard it.

"Maybe it was my imagination," she whispered, feeling the pulse beating quickly in her throat. She tapped the signal again, her ear pressed against the door. The sound came back, though fainter than before.

dot-dot-dot, dash-dash-dash, dot-dot-dot

Now what to do? As she hesitated outside the door, her ear caught the faint sound, around the corner and down the hall, of the elevator doors sliding open.

Panic seized her. If it was the kidnappers coming back, she could not let them catch her. What excuse could she give if they found her standing outside the door? She ducked across the hall to the door with the lighted "Stairs" sign over it, opened it, slid through, and shut it behind her. Her throat felt tight with fear as she stood close to the door, straining to hear any sound. She knew the thick hall carpet would muffle any footsteps until they were right outside the door, but maybe whoever was coming would be talking and would give a clue to who they were. If she heard someone jangling keys outside that apartment, would she dare open the stairway door a crack to see who it was? She would have to. It would be awful to miss out on a chance to describe the kidnappers to the police.

But though she strained to hear, no sound at all came from the hallway. She felt trapped. Had someone come along so noiselessly that she had not heard? Then a worse thought petrified her. Had someone caught a glimpse of her slipping through the stairway door? And was he now just standing there waiting for her to make a false move and come out?

Then the sudden roar of a machine in the hall made her jump. But almost immediately she relaxed, feeling weak with relief. It was just the maintenance man vacuuming the hall carpet. The noise got louder, which meant he was coming down this side of the floor and would come clear to the end of the hall, past the stairway exit where she was standing, and reach to 1492B.

Should she tell him what she suspected about the apartment and ask him to open the door? She shook her head. No. Maintenance men in their building were not allowed to unlock apartment doors unless the occupants gave permission. She had no proof that the little boy was in there. No proof she could show to anyone, because the signs in the window were all she had to go on. Anyway, there was still the chance that she could rescue the little boy herself if she just had a little more time.

She hoped the maintenance man would not open the stairway door and find her there. She could give him some excuse, of course, about why she was just standing there, but she did not want him to remember her. To make sure she would not be discovered, she went halfway up the stairs to the next landing, ready to scurry farther up out of sight if necessary. But as she waited and listened, the vacuuming noise gradually receded along the hall and she knew he was going to the other side of the hall.

Finally the roar stopped. If they did things here the way they did in her building, he would take the big vacuum machine to the next floor, either up or down. She stayed where she was to give him time to ring for the service elevator.

When she was sure he had gone and had left the floor quiet again, she pulled open the stairway door and hurried across to 1492B. She tapped the signal again and stood listening. No answer came back. She reached for the door knob, turning it carefully, but the door was locked as she was sure it would be.

She chewed her lip, wondering what to do, her mind turning over all the clues. The kidnappers must have been gone a few minutes ago when she tapped the signal, or the little boy would not have dared respond. No one had come in the meantime. Then why didn't he reply to her now? The answer was obvious. He knew they would be back any minute and by not answering he was warning her to leave.

The best thing to do was to go home and plan her next move. She hurried to the elevator, glad when it came almost immediately, glad that no one else was on it. She had not seen—or been seen by—anyone, which would give her clear access the next time she came over.

When she went through the lobby, Charlie

58

stopped her, his friendly face beaming. "Did you find your friend?"

She gave him a quick smile in return, sort of half-nodded at him, and pushed on through the revolving doors. A guilty feeling nagged at her. Even though she had not really said yes to his question, she had given the impression of yes. That was one trouble with the detective business. How could you be completely honest and still keep secret what had to be kept secret until you were free to tell about it after you had successfully completed a case?

She stepped out into the sun's glare, thinking of how, as far back as she could remember, her parents had drummed into her the awfulness of lying. Dad harped on it all the time. She could understand why he felt that way, of course. In his business he met people who lied all the time.

"Half the messes people get themselves into come from not being honest, from not telling the whole truth about what happened. A half truth is just as wrong as an out and out lie and does just as much damage," he insisted.

Vickie remembered how her mother had challenged him once, saying, "Now, Carl, sometimes you have to tell a half truth in order to be kind."

He shook his head in answer. "I don't believe you can document that."

"All right. I'll prove it. Wait a minute."

Mrs. Montgomery hurried out of the room and returned with one of her red and blue and purple landscapes. She propped the painting on a chair across the room from him and stood with folded arms.

"Now tell me—with complete honesty, of course—what you think of it."

He laughed and winked at Vickie before he answered. "You think you have me trapped so that I'll have to say either 'I don't like it,' and hurt your feelings, or else say 'I like it' and lie, since you know this is not my idea of art."

"Well?" she challenged.

"I have a third choice," he answered.

"What?"

"I can frankly say that I prefer a picture to be a recognizable something—a tree or a house or a vase of flowers. But since you see beauty in some other form, I respect your opinion. After all, you don't recognize the beauty in a carefully worked out, logically developed argument in a trial case, but I'm glad you let me appreciate it. So you see, I don't have to lie about your picture just to be kind. I can just as easily tell the truth."

Vickie remembered how her mother had laughed and hugged him as she said, "I hope our girls have inherited your ability to use words to get themselves out of a tight situation without having to resort to an out and out lie."

Vickie crossed the courtyard while these thoughts jostled around in her mind, walked through the lobby, and rode up the elevator. Now she was faced with trying to keep from lying to all sorts of people while she tried to figure out how to handle this case.

When she closed the apartment door behind her, she went straight to the den and lifted the binoculars out of the desk drawer, shutting her eyes and mind against the paper-clipped pages that talked about somone who claimed to be God, someone who knew everything you thought.

She had used the binoculars already without permission, so another time would not matter. She crossed into the sunny dining room and over to the window, adjusting the binoculars to bring the other window into sharp focus. Nothing over there showed that a mystery existed. The shade was in an even line, no white paper with large black S O S or H E L P was plastered against the glass. Nothing at all indicated that a frightened, helpless six-year-old was trapped there all alone.

"But that doesn't mean he isn't there."

She found herself talking out loud about this case to reassure herself. She was more positive than ever that he was over there. In addition to the window signs, she had the evidence of actually having heard the tapped-out signal.

With all this evidence the really smart thing to do now was to get help from someone. She had better call the police after all. Then, if they did not believe her, rescuing Andy would be up to her. She went to the kitchen and dialed swiftly, before she could change her mind.

When the phone was answered, she could hear a lot of commotion in the background before a gruff voice said, "Police Emergency. Officer Brown."

"Hello? I have some information about the kidnapped boy." She tried to make her voice sound grown-up, but instead heard it squeak, and she cleared her throat.

"What kind of information?"

"Well—first there was this crooked window

shade. I—I was eating breakfast yesterday and first it was straight like always and then it was crooked. Then last night I saw lights flashing off and on—like a signal, you know? And then I saw—"

"Where did you see all this?" he interrupted, his voice curt.

"In an apartment building on Linden Boulevard—"

"OK, thanks." The phone clicked.

Vickie hung up. He had not believed her. But then, could she blame him? She should have planned how to give the evidence instead of blurting it all out in a jumble.

She walked back to the dining room window, angry at herself for making such a mess. *"I'll never make a lawyer,"* she muttered.

This meant it was going to be up to her to help the little boy. Well, after all, she argued silently, she was the one to whom he was appealing for help. Nobody else was paying any attention to his silent, written cries. Somehow he watched for her and put his pitiful pleas for help into his window for her to answer.

Suddenly aware of how ravenous she was, she went out to the kitchen to fix a sandwich to help her work out the problem. Then, glancing at the clock, she knew why her stomach was rattling. It was already one o'clock.

"Hey, maybe there'll be news on television, and they'll say something about the kidnapping."

She grabbed a tray and piled on a sandwich, a stack of potato chips, half a dozen chocolate chip cookies, and an apple, and carried it into the den.

62

She snapped on the TV and sat down cross-legged on the floor.

Sure enough, the kidnapping was the first news report. The announcer reviewed all the developments, his voice pounding out the news in clipped, urgent tones, but said he had nothing new to report. The police were investigating every lead, following up every phone call and every letter. Even anonymous calls were being investigated.

"Oh, yeah!" Vickie said to the TV set. "They don't even believe the calls."

The announcer went on, "All the TV channels are cooperating with a special number to call. So if you know of anything that looks suspicious that might have a bearing on the case, please call this number. Remember, little Andy's life may depend on you."

The number stayed on the screen long enough for Vickie to memorize it. But just to be sure she would not forget it, she got pencil and paper and wrote it down. She went to her room and slipped the paper under a stack of sweaters in a bottom dresser drawer. Then she went back to the den and switched off the TV.

She thought about the announcer's plea for information while she finished the sandwich and munched the potato chips. She picked up the apple, rubbing it in her hands, trying to decide what to do.

It would not hurt to call the number and try to convince someone else that she knew something— provided it was not Officer Brown who answered again. She could give more definite information this time, since anonymous meant she would not have to give her name.

Of course, that would mean she would not get the credit for saving Andy. The thought brought regret, but deep down she knew that that was not the important thing.

A thought still nagged when she let it. Someone definitely was in trouble in that apartment. *But could she be sure it was Andy?* She had never actually seen him—

The thought made her stop, and she frowned over it. It was strange that she saw the messages but not the person who put them there. Still, the notes in the window and the response to her SOS signal had to be done by someone. The more she thought about it, the more sure she was that it was Andy. The kidnapping and the sudden pleas for help had come too close together for it to be accidental.

The scraping sound of a key turning in the lock made her freeze in panic. It was too early for Mother to be home. She realized how ragged her nerves were from thinking so much about the kidnappers.

Then a voice said, "Yoo-hoo," and Vickie relaxed. Of course. Anna always came to clean the apartment on Tuesday.

That clicked a light in her mind. What more logical way to get information about who lived in other apartments than from a cleaning person. Someone who cleaned in a couple of apartments would know the "inside dope" on a lot of others. Maybe. Anyway it was worth a try. But she would have to go after her information carefully and not let on to Anna what she suspected.

She jumped up and went out to the kitchen where Anna had already spread out scrubbing equipment and dusting cloths.

"Hi, Anna. Mother said I'm supposed to clean all the kitchen drawers and then do anything else you want me to help you with."

"So. Your mama is wise. Your mama is the only one of all the mamas I work for that wants her daughter to know how to clean a house. It is good."

"Yeah. Well, maybe you and she think it's a good idea, but I don't," Vickie answered in pretended disgust.

"You will be glad some day," Anna answered.

She took a tightly sealed jar from a paper sack. "I promised your mama to tell how to make cabbage soup. So I bring some for your supper."

"*Cabbage* soup?"

"Do not say, '*cabbage* soup' and wrinkle your nose. Wait to taste!" Anna's voice was stern as she put the jar in the refrigerator.

Vickie got a pan of water and a sponge, splashed in a cleaning solution, and began taking knives and forks out of the drawers. She looked around at Anna.

"How many apartments do you clean?"

"Two in a day. One in the morning, one in the afternoon. That is all I have time for if I am to clean good."

She worked while she talked, her arms and mouth keeping time in vigorous motion. "Some

65

who clean do not know what it is to clean house. Do they move the chairs from the wall and clean behind? No! Do they polish the beautiful window sills and the doorknobs? No! Do they clean the lightbulbs in all the fancy lamps so they shine good? No! For them it is enough to wipe a sponge on the kitchen floor and push a cleaner on the thick rugs."

"Are there lots of ladies like you who clean?"

"There are lots who *say* they clean."

Vickie could tell Anna was still huffy on the subject. She would have to try to get her information another way. She waited a few minutes until Anna came back by the kitchen and asked her, "Do you clean in the other building too?"

Anna shook her head. "No. All my ladies are only in this building. I could have jobs there, but I do not have time for more. I cannot clean four houses in one day the way some say they can," she said, her voice showing her scorn.

She dusted a table carefully as she talked, wiping the polish on with broad, even strokes until the gleaming wood surface reflected Vickie's watching face.

"Do you know anyone who does?"

"Does what?"

"Cleans in the other building?"

"Yah, I know one."

Anna disappeared into the den and Vickie heard the whir of the vacuum cleaner. She hurried to the dining room window and stood close to the glass so she could be seen. No sign was in the other window and none appeared. The vacuum was still humming in the den, which meant

Anna was still there. Vickie waved the cloth she had used to wipe the drawers dry and waited, hoping for an answer. None came.

Anna spoke from behind her. "So you are through so soon? We will see." She went into the kitchen, pulled open drawers, and ran her fingers into the corners of the dividers.

"Better you should have used more soap and water. More—how is it my boy says?—more elbow grease. Now you must polish the silverware before it goes back. To be clean, it must all be clean. I fix you here while I scrub clean the floor."

Vickie took the jar of silver polish and slowly spread a generous amount down the length of a knife. She listened to Anna talk over the sound of the brush swishing back and forth over the tile floor.

"I guess your mama does not know how she could get me so quick to clean. You been here, what? Three weeks? Four? Yah, some people wait a whole year to get on a list for someone to clean. Then longer to get someone."

"Really? How come we got you so quick?"

"It is because of your papa."

Vickie looked at her with surprise. "Dad knew about you?"

"No, no. He did not know me. It goes back sometime last year. My neighbor's boy got into trouble, maybe a year ago. It was not all his fault, but some of it was. I keep telling my neighbor she should know more where he is, what he does away from home, who he runs with. She would not listen."

Anna's voice receded as she moved in to clean

the living room windows, and Vickie followed her, a fork clutched in one hand and the polishing cloth in the other.

"Anyway, it is not all her fault. She had no one to help when her husband died. So when Tony got in trouble, she went to the police station, but no one sees her. How can it be that someone is there and no one sees? Everybody run, run, run. Too busy to help. They see papers but not people. When it came to his trial, she went and sat all day on a bench. No one told her anything. She sat so one day, two days. No one looked at her. No one answered the questions she asked."

Anna stopped to shake her head. "She not talk good English like I do. She not know how to ask questions right. The third day she is sitting on the bench, crying. She hear someone walking but she not look up. For why should she? No other one had stopped to say, 'Is it help I can give?' Then she is staring at polished shoes standing before her. She could not believe when she heard, 'Can I help you?'"

Anna looked around at Vickie and nodded her head. "Yah, it was your papa. When she told him about her boy, your papa knew how to ask questions. He found out all about him. Oh, yah. Tony was guilty. But he had not before done wrong, so your papa got him free. Not all free. It would not be good for him to be all free and your papa knows that. Tony must go once every month to the policeman to tell him where he is, what he does. Your papa helped him find a job for after school and Saturday, but he must stay in school."

Anna stood, her arms on her hips, shaking her head. "That papa of yours. Anybody helps important people, people who give back something. Only good men, great men, help people not important. Your papa is a great man."

Vickie followed her as she moved into the bathroom to polish the mirrors, and asked, "But what does that have to do with your coming here to clean? We didn't live here then."

"I wrote down your papa's name when my neighbor tells what he did for her. I say to myself, 'Anna, some day you need help you go to him.' I hope I do not need help but if I do, I go to him. Then one day I read about your mama in the paper. About her showing pictures she has made. I go one day and look."

Anna shook her head again. "I did not see pictures that look like pictures of things I know. But if your mama say they are pictures, they are pictures. Next I read that you move into the city. Into my building. I tell my neighbor I clean for you. Your mama could find no one better. So I say thank you to your papa for how he helped my neighbor, my friend."

She looked at Vickie and nodded her head for emphasis. "I do not work for everybody. For some of the fancy ladies in this building, I would not step into the door. One big, so-rich lady sold some fancy rings and then said they were stolen. By the cleaning lady!" Her voice spit the words out in scornful anger.

"Why would she do that?"

"For to have insurance money and the money she got paid for. I learn some people look fancy on the outside, but the inside is not always the same. Your papa now. You be like him when you grow up. Always helping people, your papa is."

Vickie grabbed at the opening that came so unexpectedly. She said quickly, "Anna, I have to ask you something. I have to find out about someone who lives in the other building. I think someone over there needs help. But I can't tell anyone about it yet," she added hastily, seeing the question in Anna's eyes.

"It is what apartment?"

"This one." She led Anna to the dining room window and pointed out the windows. "See? It's the one with the red geraniums on the balcony. The number is 1492B."

Anna shook her head. "I do not know the number. You want I should find who lives there?"

"Can you do it sort of quietly? Without letting on to anyone that someone might need help?"

Anna nodded vigorously. "No problem. Cleaning ladies know things. I will ask."

"And can you find out real soon? It's—it's very important." Vickie could not keep the worried sound out of her voice and Anna looked at her sharply.

"You cannot ask your papa to help?"

"Not yet. First I have to find out something myself. Please call me."

Anna reached over and patted her shoulder. "Before I go home today, I will tell you what I know," she promised.

70

6

After Anna left, Vickie prowled through the house restlessly, making frequent trips to look across at the blank windows across the courtyard. She looked at the clock in each room as she wandered through it, and tried to will the clock hands to move more slowly, to give Anna more time to ask questions. Had she been positive enough to Anna that she needed to know right away?

It was already almost four, which meant her mother would be home any minute. She usually stayed beyond the time she expected to, because something unavoidable and terribly interesting always detained her at the last minute. But if she came home on time today and answered the phone, she would wonder what Anna was talking about. And then she would ask questions that Vickie was not prepared to answer yet.

Vickie paced back and forth from the phone in the den to the bedroom and kitchen extensions, her hands clenched, muttering, "Anna, please call. Hurry."

She had no idea what she would do if, when Anna called, she said no one lived in that apartment, that it was completely empty. Then how could the messages be explained?

The phone rang and she dashed for it in the kitchen just as she heard a key turn in the lock of the front door and her mother's lilting voice call, "Vickie, I'm home."

71

She grabbed the phone, turned her back to the open doorway and whispered, "Hello?"

"This is Anna. I cannot hear you."

"Did you find out anything?" She kept her voice at a low whisper.

"There is nothing I know. The doorman says they are new people. He does not know them. He was not here when they moved in. They go in the morning early and come home late. You want I should ask something more?"

"No. Thanks, Anna. Thanks a lot."

She put the phone down, feeling triumphant. No wonder the doorman knew nothing about them. Kidnappers would not want anyone to know about them. She turned nonchalantly as her mother came into the kitchen.

"I guess you didn't hear me come in. Was the phone for me?"

"No. Wrong number I guess."

The lie slipped out so easily it was said before Vickie could bite it back. It proved Dad was right, she thought uneasily. He said one lie usually led to another and the second one was always easier to tell than the first one. But she reminded herself that these lies were necessary. She could not let her mother know what was happening. Not yet. Not until she had more evidence.

She listened as her mother explained, "Sorry I'm a little later than I intended. The most interesting couple came in just as I was ready to leave and they asked such intelligent questions about my paintings that I simply had to talk to them. I can't wait to tell your father the comments they made. They saw elements in my paintings that even I didn't know were there." She laughed at herself as she spoke and went into her studio to unpack her portfolio of sketches.

Vickie trailed after her, only half listening. Her mind was too full of her own problem.

She kept worrying, *What shall I do? What will happen to that poor little kid if he isn't rescued soon? It could be dangerous for me to go over there all by myself. I really should tell Mother and Dad about him.*

But she was sure her mother would say, "Now, Vickie, that's your imagination again. Remember the time you were so sure someone had broken into the Robinson's house that summer they were away in Europe that you persuaded me to report it to the police? And when the police came to investigate, they found that relatives had come during the night with a key to the house and were expecting to stay there. The Robinsons just hadn't thought to mention it to us. And remember the time you were absolutely sure Sandy's bike had been stolen, when actually she had loaned it to the girl you saw riding it. Not to mention the scare you gave us when you insisted Pam's baby sister had swallowed a penny. And she hadn't. Your interest in helping people is commendable. The problem is that sometimes it becomes simply meddling in other people's business."

Vickie had heard that so often she could practically hear her mother saying the words now. Only this time she would say them even more positively and forbid her to have anything to do with that apartment. That would mean deserting the little boy. But she had to do something. She had tried the police, and Officer Brown had not believed her. So probably the TV number was the next thing to try.

She made the decision while she half listened to her mother's lighthearted recital of all the interesting things that had happened to her that day. She was so busy with her own thoughts that she did not realize her mother had stopped talking and was looking at her with a contrite expression.

"I'm sorry, Vickie. I'm rattling on this way and not even asking what you did all day. Did you sleep late? Swim? If not, we could take a quick dip before dinner." Her voice ended on a questioning note and Vickie shook her head.

"Nah, I don't want to now. I will tomorrow."

"I can tell Anna has been here because there is the marvellous clean smell she always leaves behind her."

"She left a better smell in the refrigerator," Vickie said. "But I'm not sure I want to try it. It's cabbage soup."

"You mean she brought a sample?" Mrs. Montgomery pulled open the refrigerator door, unscrewed the top of the jar, and sniffed the contents.

"Umm, looks good. But I didn't expect her to bring some. The recipe would have been enough."

"She said she wanted you to try it first because she puts in extra spices and stuff."

"I can't wait to taste it. Vickie, if you don't want to swim, I'd appreciate your help with dinner."

"What are we having?"

"Well, the cabbage soup won't go with the meal

I had planned, but let's have it first anyway. I thought we'd do shrimp and chicken crepes."

"Super! Can we have ice cream crepes with peanut butter chocolate sauce for dessert?"

"You may fix one for yourself, but spare the rest of us, please. I'll settle for sherbet."

Vickie watched her mother rub the back of her neck in a tired gesture. "I've stood so long in front of that easel today that I feel frozen in that position. Let me just run in and shower and change and then I'll come help."

Vickie waited until she heard the bathroom door close and the sound of the shower. Then she dashed to her bedroom and yanked open the drawer where she had hidden the number the TV announcer gave. She hurried back to the kitchen extension and dialed quickly, listening impatiently as the phone rang at the other end of the line. She did not have much time to get the call through. Her mother could zip in and shower and be out in the time it took most people to decide whether they were going to shower. She thought the water had stopped so she hung up quickly and listened.

It was still running, so she dialed again and this time someone answered almost immediately.

"Hello?"

Vickie cleared her throat, wanting to make her voice sound deep and old. Before she could reply, the voice impatiently repeated, "Hello?"

"I have some information about the kidnapped boy."

She waited, hearing the echo of the nervous strangeness in her voice.

"Go on."

"He is being held in an apartment."

"Where?"

"On Linden Boulevard."

She could hear her voice suddenly squeak high, and her inner excitement made the words jerky.

"Who is this?"

Suddenly aware of the quiet in her mother's bathroom, she said, "This is an *anonymous* call." She tripped over the word in her hurry to get it said. They weren't supposed to ask who it was. She hung up in panic, wondering if they had had time to trace the number. What would she do if the police came and asked who had made the call.

She had yanked out a cookbook and flipped to the section on crepes by the time her mother came out to the kitchen in a robe, toweling her hair dry.

"Do you want to try making the crepes yourself?"

"Sure. I'll fix the batter if you'll do the fillings."

Vickie looked up at the clock, wondering how long it took before they started to investigate anonymous tips. She got out flour and eggs and milk and put them into the blender, her hands moving automatically as though they were separate from her mind.

How would the police begin to search when they got the word about the child being on Linden? Linden Boulevard was a long street with lots of buildings. Would they go from building to building? Would they go into each apartment? Did the police have a right just to come to everyone's door and demand to be let in?

If the police did go from one place to the next, they would take forever to get to the right one.

And besides, the kidnappers would hear about it. She had been dumb not to be more specific. Why hadn't she said right out which apartment building it was?

Maybe she could still do it. She tiptoed cautiously to the kitchen door and heard the blow dryer going in the master bedroom. Hurrying to the phone, she dialed the station number again. As soon as the "Hello?" came, she said, "In the 1500 block on Linden," and slammed the receiver down. There. Now the police could go straight to the right building and not have to search for it.

Francine blew in just at five-thirty, her hair tumbled, her face lighted with the excitement of her day, her eyes sparkling as she whirled into the kitchen, lifting lids from the pans and peeking into the oven.

"Crepes! Neat! It's a good thing Pete couldn't make it for dinner. He doesn't think he's eaten if he hasn't had a steak—or at least a hamburger."

She disappeared into her bedroom to zip out of her skirt into jeans, talking in exclamation points the whole time.

"I am in positively the most exciting job in the whole world! Guess what anonymous tip came in today—no, you couldn't possibly guess. There were about fifteen altogether, but this one just came in about an hour ago. It said that little Andy is being held in a building on Linden Boulevard."

"*Our* Linden Boulevard?" Mrs. Montgomery asked.

"Is there any other?"

"Are they going to investigate?" Vickie hoped

her voice sounded nonchalant. To her own ears it was quavery and squeaky.

Francine nodded. "Oh, definitely. They can't afford to ignore any call no matter how far out it seems. But imagine! Linden Boulevard. Why, people like us live on Linden Boulevard."

"People like us, as you put it, are just as likely to be criminals as anyone else," her mother answered firmly.

"Well, yes. But—" Francine's eyes sparkled as she looked at Vickie and her mother. "I didn't tell you the clincher. The person identified the address—1500 Linden."

"But—but that's this block. Our building. It takes up the whole block," Mrs. Montgomery protested.

Francine nodded. "Our building or the one across the courtyard."

"I can't believe it—"

"Remember, Mother. 'People like us are just as likely to be criminals as anyone else.' " Francine's voice was colored with laughter as she quoted her mother's words.

Vickie watched her mother sweep her arms out in a wide gesture. "How will they ever track it down? There must be three hundred apartments in the two buildings. Will policemen come to each one and search it?"

That was Vickie's question and she waited for Francine's answer. But Francine shook her head, her voice doubtful. "Someone said they have different ways of following leads depending on how serious they think the lead is. Some of the tips are so way out that it doesn't take long to discover they are fake."

"Was it a man who called?" Mrs. Montgomery asked.

Francine shook her head again. "We don't know. Walt answered the phone. He's the one they've assigned to handle the calls. He said he couldn't tell. The person was definitely trying to disguise his voice."

"Did the person sound the same both times?"

As soon as Vickie asked the question, she knew how dumb she had been. Francine had not said anything about two calls. Her mind raced frantically, trying to think of some way to explain how she knew there had been two calls. But the question, which had sounded so loud in her own ears, went unnoticed as Francine bubbled on, her smile bursting out.

"Isn't this the craziest development? I told Pete about it on the way home and he said he didn't think there was anything to it. He said it was probably a poor little old lady who wanted some excitement in her drab life and had just picked this address out of the blue."

She sobered then and added, "The thing is it's terrible to pretend something that isn't true when this is such a serious case."

Vickie turned away so they could not see her face. She pinched her lips together to keep from saying, "But it is true. It is!"

She let the conversation swirl around her as Francine repeated the story to her father at the dinner table. Because they always ate dinner at the big table in the center of the dining room instead of at the little one by the plant-filled window, Vickie could not see the window in the other apartment. She gulped her milk so she could get more and casually looked out the window when she stood up. If only a huge plea for help would appear, she could point it out. Then the whole family would see something was wrong over there. But there was no change in the empty look of the other window.

Time dragged that evening as she stewed around. She could not get interested in TV or in a book. How could a made-up story compare with what was happening so close to her? She wondered when the police would start checking the building and what she would say if they came to their apartment to ask if anyone had information about the kidnapping. The rest of the family would say no. She would have to say yes.

Because she tossed restlessly half the night, lifting her head to see the clock hands move from twelve to one and then to two before finally dozing off, she slept late the next morning. Everyone was gone when she got up. The usual note, with the funny little drawings her mother always did to make it more interesting, was propped against the toaster. This one had a polar bear diving into a snowbank and the little caption said, "Try it, you'll like it."

> Get some swimming in today, honey. It's good exercise, it will give you something to do, and it will cool you off. You looked a little tense and upset yesterday. Sorry to leave you alone again. Will do my best to be home by three *sharp*.

She was tense today, too, and kept spilling co-
coa and dripping the milk from her cereal as she
tried to eat without taking her eyes away from the
opposite window. She had decided Andy somehow knew when she was at the table eating breakfast because the signs from him had come about
this time yesterday and the day before. But today
the window stayed empty.

After she cleared the breakfast dishes to the
dishwasher, she prowled the house restlessly, going from one window to the next, and peering
down into the courtyard. There was no sign that
the police were around.

She stopped abruptly. How dumb! Naturally
the police would not come around so they would
be seen. That would tip off the kidnappers. They
would come as—what were they called?—plain-
clothesmen, police dressed in ordinary clothes,
not uniforms. They could be anybody.

She rushed to the dining room window and
looked down into the courtyard. A mother and
two little girls stood watching the fountain sparkle
in the sun. A boy rode his tricycle around and
around the tree-lined walks. An older man sat
on a bench reading a newspaper. There was absolutely nothing suspicious there at all.

She started to turn away, discouraged, when she
suddenly realized that the man was acting in a
strange way. He was reading the newspaper, or
at least it looked as though he was. But then he
slowly lowered it slightly, and Vickie could see
that he was looking over the top of the paper.
Then he raised it to eye level again and, after several minutes, lowered it and peeked over the top.

81

Excitement flared within her. She thought policemen would be younger than that. But of course if he just sat on a bench as a lookout, his age would not matter. They probably chose the most experienced men for that kind of job, men who knew what to do in an emergency.

She watched, fascinated, as he pretended to read the paper but kept alert to what was going on around him. Then worry nagged her. If she, so inexperienced in detective work, could tell that he was a plainclothesman, would real criminals not spot him too?

Her eyes caught a flicker of movement from behind a low bushy tree at the edge of the stone wall that circled the fountain. She watched a little girl run from behind the bush and stand looking up at the man. He dropped his paper and Vickie saw them laughing at each other. Then the man stood up and walked off, holding the little girl's hand and carrying a rag doll by one leg. He was just a grandfather playing hide and seek with his granddaughter. So much for her imagination.

She had wasted all this time and was no nearer what to do than she had been yesterday. Maybe the doorman had been alerted to the possibility of the police's coming. He might let some information slip if she went down and talked to him as she looked for the mail.

When she got to the lobby, Vickie saw Mac standing at the door, looking out into the courtyard. She strolled over to stand beside him.

"What's going on? I thought I saw a policeman out there."

She felt only a little guilty saying the half truth, because she *had* thought the old man was a police officer.

Mac laughed as he shook his head. "Nah. We don't have policemen coming around us. Some places may need them, but we have such nice people living in these buildings that we never have to call for help."

That's what you think, Vickie said silently and went to the bank of mailboxes.

There was no mail for her. All her friends had forgotten her, wiped her completely out of their thoughts. Even Betty Lou, best friend since nursery school sandbox days, had written only one stingy little letter. She went back upstairs, dragged her feet along the carpeted hall, and let herself into the silent apartment. Since there was nothing else to do, she might as well eat an early lunch and then go swimming. That would at least pass the time.

But as she ate, she could not keep her mind off the other apartment, wondering what was happening over there behind those windows that looked so harmless. She finished a peanut butter and honey sandwich, an apple, and a piece of chocolate cake and sat staring out the window.

A white paper was suddenly plastered against the opposite window glass. It was larger this time, larger than the other signs, and it had new words that she could read easily.

PLEASE HURRY

Vickie ran to her room, dug in her closet for

school poster paper, grabbed a thick black crayon, and printed an answer in large letters.

AM TRYING TO HELP

She rushed back and stuck it against the window, holding it flat against the glass. She watched anxiously for some other word, or some sign that Andy had seen her reply. There was none. Only the paper remained in the window, the words a heartbreaking cry for help.

Now what should she do? She had to do something definite to help. She whirled, dug from under the stack of sweaters the slip of paper with the phone number, and dialed the number again. As soon as the man answered, she said abruptly, "That little boy *is* in the building on Linden Boulevard."

She made her voice sound deep and positive, and then listened as the person on the other end said, "Wait a minute."

He either covered the receiver with his hand or turned his head, because his words were indistinct.

". . . nut who called . . . Andy in apartment . . . Insists Linden." Someone in the background said something and Vickie heard him reply, "OK," as his voice came back.

"Um, listen. Tell me more about it, will you?"

"I've told you all I know."

"Well, can't you give me an exact address? Something more definite?"

"I said the 1500 block."

"Yeah, I know." His voice was relaxed, patient. "But there are a lot of apartment buildings out that way. It takes a long time to go through all of them."

Vickie panicked, realizing he was stalling for time. Maybe this time they really were going to trace the call. She started to hang up. Then, as she stood just inside the dining room with the phone cord stretched full length, she saw the white paper with its urgent plea.

PLEASE HURRY

She had to say something that would let them know this was not just a crank call. It had to be something that would make them take the call seriously and send the police to search. Otherwise she would have to undertake the dangerous rescue attempt all alone.

"Ask Francine Montgomery," she blurted and slammed down the receiver.

As soon as the words were out she wanted to snatch them back. She never should have said them. She had involved Francine in something Francine knew nothing about. Would she guess that Vickie was the one who had phoned?

The rest of the afternoon went by in a daze of worry. She flipped the television on to a silly program just to keep her mind occupied. When it was over, she deliberately refrained from looking out the window. She had taken down her sign and closed her eyes to Andy's plea.

When her mother came home, she answered questions about her day with a recital of things she had done, some of which were not true. Now there seemed no way to stop lying.

As she set the table for dinner, she saw that the sign was gone from Andy's window. The kidnappers must be there. She wondered where he was able to hide the signs and the paper and crayons so they would not find them. All the news reports stressed what an unusually sensible and resourceful child he was—old for his years. Somehow he had figured out a way to fool the kidnappers.

Francine was as upset as Vickie had known she would be when she burst into the apartment just before dinner with Pete trailing her.

"Honestly, that—that nut!" she exploded.

The words brought everyone into the wide front hall, with Vickie standing well behind her parents.

"Who are you talking about?" Mr. Montgomery asked.

"That person who called yesterday about little Andy being held on Linden Boulevard. He called back today and said that *I* knew all about it. I don't know how he—she—whoever—even got my name!"

"When did this happen?" her mother demanded.

"Just this afternoon. He called and said the same thing he had before about Andy being on Linden. Then when Walt asked for more information, he said, 'Ask Francine Montgomery,' and hung up."

I guess I really did disguise my voice, Vickie thought with relief when she heard Francine keep saying "he."

But then Mr. Montgomery asked, "It was a man who called?"

"Well, they aren't sure. Walt thinks it's a kid

trying to sound grown up." Francine shrugged her impatience at unimportant questions. "But what I want to know is why he picked on me?"

"Perhaps he saw you on the news when they've given reports about it," her father suggested.

Pete broke in. "Yeah. You do stand out in a crowd you know."

"But my name?" she insisted.

"You always give it. 'This is Francine Montgomery, reporting from the scene of the crime.'"

Pete's grin flashed as he quoted, but it faded when Mrs. Montgomery broke in, her voice quick and agitated.

"I knew something like this would happen, Francine. I knew you were going to be badgered by all the psychological goofs who follow all the murders and other crimes—"

"Now, Louise, calm down," Mr. Montgomery interrupted.

But Francine protested, "I'm not bothered just because someone knows my name. The problem is that the staff, the guys in the news room, think I really do know something and that I'm not telling them because I'm trying for a scoop."

"Francine, they don't really think that. They're just teasing you."

But Francine, near tears, shook off Pete's reassurance. "This isn't something to tease about. Here this poor little kid has been held by kidnappers for what? Four days? His parents are frantic, waiting for news about him. And suddenly it turns into something to joke about, something for every crackpot in the city to phone in silly tips about. He could be lying dead some place while we waste time like this."

Vickie stood on the edge of the conversation, wanting to say, "Francine, he isn't dead and the tip is real, even though including you was dumb."

But she could not say anything. They would laugh at the idea of messages in the window coming only when she was home alone to see them. She went to the dining room window and looked out, wanting desperately to see the black, pleading SOS sign. But there was nothing.

Pete stayed for dinner, but left right after dessert. At the table they had not been able to talk of anything else. When Pete had gone, Francine said, "I'm going to turn in. I've got to get some sleep and be ready for all the flack I'll get about this tomorrow."

Vickie trailed along the hall to Francine's room and perched on the edge of the bed, watching her brush her hair.

"Francine. Francine, if you—if you know something—something sort of secret, should you tell?"

"It depends on what the secret is and who else is involved. If it isn't your secret alone, then it isn't yours to tell."

Vickie sat silently, studying the sparkling crystal jars and bottles on Francine's dressing table. That answer really did not help much, because this was a secret that had to be told for the safety of the other person. But she knew the thing that kept her from telling her parents was a nagging fear that she might be wrong after all. She had been wrong so many other times when she had imagined someone needed help and it turned out they did not.

And anyway, she thought, *I have tried and nobody believes me.*

While she sat on the bed, tracing the design of the bedspread with her finger, she realized that Francine was watching her in the huge mirror. Then Francine put down her hairbrush and turned to face Vickie, her expression serious and loving.

"Vickie, I'm afraid the rest of us have been very selfish. Mother and Dad and I talked a lot about you before wc moved in here. We wondered what the move would do to your life. You know it has been great for us. We really haven't had any trouble adjusting to life in the city. In fact, it's made things easier for us. Dad is closer to the office and Mother is right in the middle of the art scene. And I love it. You're the one who has had to change your lifestyle, give up your friends."

"I haven't minded, Francine," Vickie protested, but even to herself her voice did not sound convincing.

"You must be lonely all day with the rest of us just going about our business as usual. We've got to help you find friends now and not wait until school starts."

Vickie felt near tears. The loneliness she had held in check, refused to admit completely to herself, rushed in on her. She had been missing someone to laugh and do fun things with, as she had done with Sandy. She also missed spending long hours hacking things over with Betty Lou. But even worse was the terrible specter of starting a new school all alone, not knowing anyone.

She wrenched her mind away from the thought and back to the mystery. That was the only thing she had to keep her from thinking about school. But the mystery was becoming so complicated that she knew she needed help in solving it. She would give it until tomorrow. Then, if nothing happened, she would tell the rest of the family all she knew about Andy.

7

Vickie woke the next morning and sniffed. Was that frying bacon she smelled? If so, it meant she was awake early and Dad was still home. Francine was strictly an orange juice and coffee breakfast person and Mother usually had only orange juice, toast, and coffee. Dad was the one who could eat cereal, eggs, pancakes, and bacon and still look like a college athlete. She yawned and stretched and rolled over to peer sleepily at the clock.

She lifted her head in surprise. 8:30? If the clock was right, and bacon frying meant Dad was still home, then he was already late to work. Most unlike him.

She grinned to herself about the detective-like thought and then sobered. It brought a reminder of the problem that loomed before her, and of the decision that she had to make today. If she waited too long, the kidnappers might get desperate and do something she could have prevented otherwise.

Right now she had better get up and fortify herself for the day with some food. She might as well dress to start with or she would be sent back to do it. That's what came of belonging to parents with rules like "Robes and slippers at the breakfast table are allowable on Christmas and birthdays only." So she pulled on clothes quickly, splashed water on her face, and combed her hair.

She went through the kitchen and into the dining room. "Well, it's not only bacon but waffles too," she said as she slid into her chair by the fern hanging in the sunny window.

She had given a quick, surreptitious glance out the window as she went around to her place at the table. Again she wished that a sign would be there so she could say, "Hey, look. Is that a message of some kind over there?" Then she could tell about the other signs and her suspicions and admit that she had made the phone call that involved Francine. Then they would understand why she had done it. But the other window was blank.

She looked from her mother to her father. "What's the celebration? Even my place is set with a fancy place mat. Though I notice you didn't wake me up."

"We didn't dare until we'd had our share of waffles," her father answered, helping himself to the hot one that was just ready.

He poured syrup over the melted butter that he had spread on the waffle as he explained, "I decided I didn't have to get to the office so early this morning. I thought I should see a little more of my family. Even Francine sat down long enough to drink a glass of juice and eat a slice of melon."

Vickie watched her mother spoon more batter into the waffle iron and listened as she said, "We've been talking about getting in a family vacation before the summer is over. Francine suggested camping. She gets a week off the first part of next month. Any place special you would like to go? You could invite someone to go along."

"Great! Maybe Betty Lou will be back by then."

"In the meantime, how about having lunch with me sometime this week?" her father asked.

Vickie looked across the table at him, her eyes sparkling. "Can we eat at your club? They have the neatest sandwiches there. You know the ones I mean? With all the layers of stuff in between the two thin slices of bread?"

Her father laughed as he put his hands up to hold his cheeks. "Are you talking about the ones you dislocate your jaw trying to get your mouth open wide enough to go around the sandwich? Sure, fine with me. How about tomorrow?"

"OK." Vickie smiled a good-bye to him as he stood up, and she nodded at her mother's, "Shall I fix you another?"

She expected her mother to get up from the table with a quick, half apologetic, "I have to run, honey. Just put your dishes in the washer."

Instead, her mother poured herself more coffee and sat back, sipping it slowly as she went on talking in a relaxed, unhurried way.

"The stores will be showing back to school clothes soon. When they do, we'll have lunch and do some shopping. You need an update on clothes now that you are out of grade school."

"OK." But as she answered she suddenly understood first her dad's invitation to lunch and now this attention from her mother. Even though they were trying to be casual about it, she was sure they were both suddenly thinking they had neglected her. Francine must have told them the conversation they had had last night. She remembered how troubled Francine's face had looked.

I guess I didn't cover my feelings very well after all, she thought.

She decided not to let on that she knew what was behind all this sudden interest in her. And, anyway, the days were not quite so empty now. This mystery was helping to fill the lonely hours. While she liberally poured syrup on a fourth waffle and helped herself to sausage and listened to her mother's shopping plans, she gave quick glances out the window whenever her mother was not looking. How Andy knew when she was not alone was part of the mystery.

She hoped her mother would go to the studio today instead of painting at home. If she were alone, she would not have to sneak around and would be freer to track down the mysterious messages.

As if in answer to her thoughts, her mother said, "Vickie, I'm sorry, but I do have to go to the studio today. I wish you could find something special to do. Can't you call someone to come in and spend the day—stay overnight perhaps?"

"I'm all right. Don't worry about me. I'll probably swim. And there's—there's stuff to do."

"Just don't go wandering about on the streets. This kidnapping has been upsetting to me. It bothered me when I called yesterday and you were not at home. I had to assume you were down at the pool. I'm suddenly realizing that we didn't think this move through carefully enough. We should have waited until nearer time for school to begin so you wouldn't be alone so much."

"I'm OK," she protested.

Vickie tried to hide her impatience while her mother dressed and gathered her sketches. She stood by the window and looked down at her as she went through the courtyard. Her slender figure looked very stylish in the fitted pantsuit, its vivid blue scarf knotted around her throat. Even at that distance, Vickie could see her short reddish blond hair gleaming in the sunlight.

She stood as close to the window glass as possible so she could be seen clearly by Andy. She started to wave and then decided not to. The worst possible thing would be to attract the kidnappers' attention.

As she waited for some sign from the other window, the phone rang loudly in the stillness of the apartment. Her mind had been so intent on what was happening across the courtyard that she ran to answer, thinking, "That's Andy!" Even as the thought came she knew it was silly. He would call his parents, not her. He had no idea who she was.

It was Pete, and as soon as she heard his voice, she was sure Francine had asked him to call her.

His voice was elaborately casual as he asked, "Hi, Vickie. Doing anything this noon?"

"Nothing but eating lunch."

"How about eating it with me? I've got an expense account that I haven't used at all this month —not that I'll put you on it," he added hastily. "The boss wouldn't understand my treating my girl's sister at his expense. But, anyway, Francine can't eat with me today. This case has got her all worked up. So I thought you would be the next best company to her. How about it?"

"Sure. Great."

"What do you feel like today? Hamburgers? Steak? Pizza?"

"Hey, pizza. Can I have it with everything? Does your expense account cover pepperoni, mushrooms, sausage and cheese?"

"I'll make my own budget stretch that far since it's for you. Meet you in the lobby of your building at—what? Twelve OK?"

"Sure."

She hung up and then stood by the phone. She wondered, *When did Francine ask Pete to ask me out to lunch?* She was sure he had not thought of it all by himself.

Well, she would not let on she had guessed what everyone was up to. It was really nice of them all to worry so about her. She had not known how to tell them just how much she missed her old life, so it was just as well Francine had caught on. This would make an opening so she could talk about how she dreaded starting a new school. When you could talk about a problem with someone else, it did not seem quite so serious.

The thought took her back to the window again. Everything looked normal. No paper sign was there begging for help. She remembered how the first sight of the sign had sort of scared her. But now, *not* seeing any sign made her uneasy. What if the kidnappers had discovered Andy's signals and had moved him somewhere else? Then a more frightening thought came. *What if they had done something to Andy so that he could not signal for help?*

She was sorry now that she had agreed to meet

Pete for lunch. Something important might happen in the hour or so she would be gone. She frowned at the thought that came again, something she had partly wondered about at other times. *Why did the messages always appear when she was alone?*

She looked around uneasily. It was as though someone over there could see everything that went on in their apartment, and could watch all their comings and goings. She backed away from the window.

Then she remembered that it was a little six-year-old needing her help, not someone of whom she had to be afraid.

"When I come back from lunch, I won't even go swimming," she told herself firmly. "I'll watch the apartment all afternoon."

Then this evening she would tell Dad about it and let him help decide what to do. Because there was no sign of the police, it meant they had not taken her tip seriously.

She started to get dressed to meet Pete but stopped, frowning. Maybe the reason no sign had come this morning was that the police had found Andy. She flipped on the TV, but heard no special news bulletin on any channel. She would have to leave before the twelve o'clock news, but she could casually ask Pete if he had heard anything.

She studied herself in the mirror. She really should have washed her hair. It looked kind of greasy. But it was too late now. Anyway, it wouldn't matter because the pizza place had no windows and was always so dimly lighted that no one could see anybody else very well. She put on a thin sleeveless blouse and shorts and got her silver chain with the key.

The phone rang as she headed toward the dining room for one last look. When she answered, Francine said, "Hi! How are you doing?"

"OK. Pete's taking me to lunch."

Francine's pretended surprise fell so flat that Vickie smiled to herself. One thing sure, Francine would never win a prize for best actress.

But here was an unexpected chance to find out something. Trying to sound unconcerned, she asked, "How are you doing? Has anyone said anything about—you know, your knowing where the little boy is?"

"That's all I've heard all morning. Everybody tries to top everyone else in wise remarks. And most of them aren't very funny. But I think I've convinced everyone, including the policeman who talked to me, that I don't know anything, that the caller just picked my name out of the blue. Well, I have to run. Have fun with Pete."

Vickie put down the receiver, feeling relieved and yet worried. She was glad Francine was off the hook. That had been dumb, dumb, dumb of her. And it was a big relief to know she would not have to admit that she had been the one who called. But if the police were not taking the tip seriously, it meant they would not be searching the building. That meant Andy would not be found. So the whole responsibility was back on her even though she did not want it. That settled it for sure. Tonight she would have to tell Dad all about it.

She put the silver chain with the key around her neck and under her blouse. Then she let herself out the door and waited to hear the lock click shut behind her. The elevator came quickly as though it had been waiting for her and she plummeted to the ground floor. Pete pushed in through the lobby's revolving door just as she got off the elevator.

"I thought we'd duck around a couple of blocks to the pizza place where Francine and I sometimes stop after she's worked late. It's too hot to be outside very long, so we'd better hustle. I didn't drive since there's no place to park."

The sun made the sidewalk so hot that Vickie could feel the heat through the thin soles of her sandals. She was glad for the blast of air-conditioned cold that hit them as they went into the dimness of the restaurant. They studied the menu in the flickering light of the hurricane candles, only half listening to the music blaring from the back room.

Across the table, Pete raised his eyebrows at her. "How much can you eat? Think the two of us can manage a large pizza?"

"Oh, easy. I can eat half," Vickie answered. "That is, if I can have a couple of large Cokes to go with it."

Pete gave the order and then leaned back against the wooden booth and smiled at her. "I'm glad I had this brainstorm. It's always more fun to eat with someone."

Vickie looked down at the table and shifted the silverware around. Without looking at Pete

99

she asked, "Was this really Francine's idea? Did she ask you to invite me?"

"What gave you that idea?" he demanded in mock anger. "Don't I get credit for my lunch invitations?"

"Well, Francine and I had a talk last night—about me. And now suddenly this morning I've had three invitations to lunch. Plus a call from Francine to see how I'm doing. Everyone all of a sudden is concerned about me—afraid that I'm lonely."

"Are you?"

"Well—yes." She said the words slowly. "Not that I've minded being by myself some of the time. I mean, I like myself—"

"That's a help," Pete broke in, a grin tugging the corners of his mouth and his eyes reflecting his laughter. Then he became serious as he answered, "OK, Francine did call and ask if I would invite you to lunch some day. But it was my idea to do it today. I didn't know you would be bombarded with so many invitations at once."

Then, looking directly at her, he added, "It has been tough on you leaving all your friends, hasn't it?"

Vickie nodded, not meeting his eyes, still fooling with the silverware.

"There's something else bothering you?" His voice made the words a question, and even though his voice was kind, it was probing.

Vickie looked across the table at him and then away quickly. Then she burst out, "It's *awful* to be born into a family where everyone else is smart

100

and talented and not be smart or talented yourself. If I were beautiful like Francine, it wouldn't be so bad. But I'm not that either and never will be."

"Who said you weren't smart, talented, or beautiful?"

Vickie looked at Pete in disgust. "If you saw my grades, some of them anyway, you would know I'm not smart. If you saw me trying to paint or do crafts or sew, you'd know I don't have any talent. I can't even play the piano so you can recognize the piece, even though I've taken lessons for almost two years. As for being beautiful —"

She stopped. Her voice cracked as she finished, "I just have to look in the mirror to see what everyone else sees whenever they look at me."

Pete looked at her thoughtfully for a minute, without answering. Then Vickie saw him reach into his inner coat pocket.

"I want to show you something, Vickie."

He pulled out his wallet, took out a picture, and handed it across to her. "It's pretty dim in here, but I think you can see this if you hold it close to the candle there."

Vickie took it and held it near the flickering flame. Then, surprise shocking her face, she stared across at Pete.

"Where did you get a picture of me? And how come you've got it in your wallet?"

His answering smile showed his amusement. "Look at it again."

She stared down at the picture. Then she ex-

101

claimed, "Why—it's not me! I have brown hair and this is a blond. And she has blue eyes. Otherwise she looks like me. Who is it?"

She looked across at him and read the answer in the smile in his eyes even before he said, "That's a picture of Francine."

Her face showed her disbelief. "Francine! This is Francine? I can't believe it!"

"But it really is. She was just about your age when the picture was taken. She doesn't know I have it so don't tell on me. We were looking at old family pictures one day and when she saw this one, she was really upset that your mother had kept it. She took it out of the album to throw it away. When she wasn't looking, I snitched it. She would really light into me if she knew I had it."

Vickie hardly heard what he was saying as she stared down at the picture, still not believing what she saw. The blond hair looked stringy. There was no other word to describe it.

Like yours does right now, a voice inside her whispered a reminder.

Francine was wearing glasses, glasses as thick as the bottom of Coke glasses. And she was hardly smiling at all. In fact, holding her mouth like that with her lips pressed together, the way Vickie knew she did sometimes, made it clear that Francine had braces on her teeth. Most incredible of all, her face was as round as a full moon. She was fat!

"She—she looks like me! But Francine doesn't look like this now. How could she change so much?"

Pete reached over and took the picture, held it, and looked down at it with a smile. "That's what time does," he answered.

"You mean, *I* will change like that too?" Vickie heard her voice end in a squeak. *"I* will look like Francine when I'm her age?"

He nodded. Then he looked at her, his expression serious. "Of course, time alone can't do it all. You have to help it a little. I'm sure Francine did."

"What do you mean?"

Pete waited until the waiter had brought the pan of pizza, served them each a thick slice, and put down the dressing-drenched salad. Then he said, "Well, eventually your braces will come off and your teeth will be straight and gleaming. And, when you are a little older, you can get contacts like Francine did. And—"

He broke off the sentence and looked at her. "Promise you won't get mad if I say something else?"

She nodded, not sure of what was coming, but knowing he was going to tell her something else that was wrong with her.

He hesitated, and she could tell he was searching for the words to say it in a nice way. After taking a good-sized bite of pizza, he wiped his mouth with his napkin and said, "Well, between us we'll probably polish off this large pizza. And on the way home, if we stopped at that new ice cream place, you'd probably order a—"

"Hot fudge sundae with nuts and whipped cream." Vickie answered the question in the unfinished sentence. The spicy pizza made her mouth welcome the thought of the smooth coolness of the ice cream.

"Yeah. But if I had Francine sitting where you are, she would eat one piece of pizza instead of three, skip the dressing on the salad, and shudder at even the thought of dessert. See what I'm getting at?"

"Oh."

Vickie chewed and swallowed the big bite of pizza, not looking at Pete. After a moment she said in a small voice. "What you mean is that I am too fat."

"I wouldn't have put it that bluntly, but, yes, you are."

Vickie leaned back. "Yeah, but food is so good. It's hard to turn it down."

Without answering, Pete dug for his wallet again and took out two pictures this time. He propped them, facing her, side by side against the basket of rolls. One was the picture he had shown her. The other was Francine's Christmas picture of last year.

"How motivated are you, Vickie?" He asked the question gently but very directly.

When she did not answer, he went on, "There's a beautiful girl like Francine hiding inside you, too. I mean a physically beautiful girl. You already are beautiful in many ways. You are thoughtful and caring like your father, fun and bubbly like your mother, considerate and sweet and dear like Francine."

He looked at her and lifted a hand in protest as she started to answer. "I really mean this, Vickie. I'm not saying all this just because I'm hoping that Francine will say yes to me some day and let me be part of your family."

He shoved his plate to one side and leaned his elbows on the table as he went on, his voice very serious.

"Maybe you're too young to know what specific talents you will be developing. Just don't worry about it and waste time wishing you could do things that maybe you never will be able to do. But, Vickie, you're not too young to start getting ready for your future. You can improve your grades by studying harder. You can play the piano better if you just make yourself practice more. And you can improve your appearance by getting your weight down, and washing and brushing your hair or whatever it is that Francine does to make hers always look so shiny. Time will do a lot for you, Vickie, but you can help it move faster."

She stared down at the remains of the pizza, feeling hurt and angry and ashamed. Yet, along with the feeling that said she could never look at Pete again, another one struggled. He showed he really cared about her. He was like an older brother looking out for her.

She looked up at him then and saw the anxious expression in his eyes as he said, "Let me finish my lecture by telling you something my grandfather used to say. He said we are what we are becoming. You already have the gifts you are going to develop. But then he said it works the other way, too. That is, we become what we are. Life is ahead of you, Vickie, and your world can be very wonderful and exciting if you help make it so."

Then his voice became embarrassed sounding as he fumbled for words. "I guess you and Francine have never gone to church from what she has told me. I haven't very much and not for a long time."

He stopped and looked across at her sympathetically as he said, "I can understand what you are going through with this move and not having any friends here. My father was in the military and we moved around a lot. I had to make friends fast when we got to each post because I knew we wouldn't be there long. One year a kid my age whom I got to know went to church and I went along, especially to Sunday school. I liked it, though I didn't learn much in just that one year. Then my father got transferred and I never went again. But the teacher we had was really big on our learning Bible verses. I wasn't much good at memorizing them, so I learned the short ones like 'God is love.' And I learned John 3:16—not the verse, which is pretty long, but the place you find it. I could always come out strong on the John 3:16 part."

"What's John 3:16? What does that mean?"

"John is the name of a book in the Bible. Three is the chapter and sixteen is the verse. The Bible is all divided into chapters and verses. John 3:16 is supposed to be the most important verse in the Bible the teacher said."

He shook his head, giving a little laugh. "That teacher would never believe I'd be explaining the

Bible to anyone—not that I'm explaining it to you now."

Vickie watched Pete as he sat shredding the straw from his Coke, a smile of past memories turning up the corners of his mouth.

Then he said, "You'll laugh at the verse I do remember. For some reason it stuck with me. I don't know where it is or what it means or anything. I was only about ten years old so it beats me why I ever remembered it. But it says, 'The king's daughter is all glorious within.' And the first time I saw Francine, that jumped into my mind. Crazy, isn't it?" he finished with an embarrassed grin. "But it does fit Francine."

Pete looked at her across the table as she sat watching and listening to his memories. "You know, Vickie, you already have a really great gift. You are an easy person to talk to because you really listen. A true friend is a person who cares enough to listen. Don't ever lose that."

His grin came back then to chase the seriousness from his face and voice. "Right now though, we can't waste this pizza. Let's finish it off, and then when we walk past the ice cream store, we'll close our eyes. OK?"

"OK. And—thanks, Pete."

8

Pete slowed his long stride to match her quick, light steps as they walked back to the apartment building. When they passed the ice cream place, its windows crammed with mouth-watering samples of three-dip cones and luscious banana splits, Pete took her elbow and laughed down at her.

"OK, Vickie. Close your eyes and I'll get you safely past temptation."

As they came into the courtyard of the apartment complex, a small boy charged toward them, furiously pedalling his trike. A wave of guilt swept Vickie. She had forgotten all about Andy because she was having such a good time.

She looked up at that important window she had been watching the last few days. If only a white paper would be there, she could casually say, "Look, Pete. I wonder why that big piece of paper is in that window," and maybe he would be curious about it too.

But the bright sun reflected in a glare on the window and made her squint her eyes, keeping her from seeing anything.

Pete walked her to the revolving doors into the lobby and said, "Thanks for keeping me from a lonely lunch." Then he waved and strode off.

Vickie watched him cross the courtyard and disappear from sight through the white iron gates. Francine was lucky to have such a neat guy wanting to marry her. She was crazy to want a career when she could snag someone as terrific as Pete. As she waited for the elevator, she thought of the picture Pete had shown her. If Francine had really looked like that when she was twelve, then there was hope for her. But Pete's warning words followed her along the hall and into the apartment. She stopped in front of the wide mirror in the hall, thinking about them.

"You've got to give time some help," he had said.

Even though he had given advice that was kind of hard to take, it was not as if he were a college graduate with a master's degree lecturing a dumb twelve-year-old. He had talked to her as though they were equals.

Vickie looked at herself in the mirror and then straightened her shoulders and pulled in her stomach. Not eating so much was going to be hard. So were some of the other things he had talked about. She walked over to the piano and ran up and down the scales a couple of times. Then she did "Mary Had a Little Lamb" with one finger. Making herself practice every day was going to be really rough.

She twirled around on the piano stool, still thinking about Pete's advice and the things he had said about himself when he was a kid. When he talked about going to church she should have told him Dad was reading the Bible. John 3:16. Why was that so important?

She jumped up and went to the den and picked up Dad's big Bible from the desk. She leafed through the pages, trying to find John. Pete had said it was a book. Then, remembering last year's library lectures about how to find what you wanted in a book, she flipped to the front and ran her finger down the list of impossible, and some

funny-sounding, names until she came to John. She found the page with John 3:16 and read the verse, "For God so loved the world, that He gave His only begotten Son, that whoever believes in Him should not perish, but have eternal life."

She read the words again, out loud this time, frowning over them. Funny, they did not *sound* so important. But Dad had written John 3:16 at the bottom of that list of—what did he call it? She hesitated a moment and then pulled open the drawer, not touching the pages, just looking at the top one with its heading, FACTS I MUST FACE ABOUT JESUS CHRIST.

Vickie looked at the list. Facts were things that were supposed to be true. But had all those things really happened? The last one—how could anyone rise from the dead? Dad never accepted anything without thinking it through carefully. Did he believe all those facts?

Then her eyes read what he had printed neatly at the very bottom of the page. "I am convinced by the evidence that Jesus Christ is God. Am I willing to accept it?"

Vickie closed the drawer quickly with the same feeling she had had before when she had looked into her father's inner self. When this mystery about Andy was solved, she would ask Dad to explain all this to her.

As she laid the Bible down, a card slipped from

inside the front cover. It was her father's business card with his name and the name of his law firm. On the back of the card in her father's neat printing were the words, "Call to Me, and I will answer you, and I will tell you great and mighty things, which you do not know" (Jeremiah 33:3).

Last year Miss Becker, had talked about how words painted pictures. *That's what these words do,* Vickie thought as she walked back to the kitchen. She automatically went to the refrigerator and reached for a candy bar and a Coke. Then, remembering Pete's words, she slammed the door hard and leaned against it.

No. She would start right now and quit eating so much. But that meant she would have to keep busy all the time so she would not think about food. Another thing would be to swim every day, doing as many laps across the pool as she could. Swimming was supposed to be the perfect exercise.

"I'll go right now."

She started for her bedroom to change and then stopped abruptly. The window! How could she forget to check the window? She turned and dashed across the dining room and looked out and felt her throat choke with excitement. Another sign appeared as soon as she got to the window, the black letters so large that she could not miss them:

S O S

She hurried to her mother's studio and got a big piece of red poster board and a thick black crayon. She printed in large strokes,

Then she rushed back and put the sign flat against the glass.

The SOS sign disappeared immediately without her seeing anyone take it. Not even a hand showed. Andy must be sitting on the floor close to the window and that was why she could never see him. She watched, anxiously, until another paper appeared. On it was only one word,

YES

Vickie took down her sign, turned it over, and printed,

HOW?

The answer came back promptly,

COME AT THREE

She backed away from the window and stretched to see the clock in the kitchen. It was one-thirty now. She scrawled,

OK

across the bottom of the poster board and put it back against the glass. The sign in the other window disappeared and, though she waited, no other message came. Finally she turned away from the window. She started to tear the poster board into small pieces to throw it away. But she stopped. The police always needed evidence. She might need this sign in case anyone thought she was making up the whole thing. She hoped Andy was keeping his signs, too. Only—could he? Did he have some place to hide them where the kidnappers would not find them? How he could signal to her without their knowing was one of the most puzzling parts of this whole mystery. He certainly was a smart little boy.

She slipped the poster board under her bed. It would be safe there until Anna came to clean next Tuesday, and by that time this whole thing would be over. This afternoon, this Thursday, she would finally solve the mystery.

She changed into her swim suit, feeling almost lighthearted. Now that the solution of the mystery was close, she did not feel the guilty responsibility that she might be making a mistake in not getting help from adults.

She could almost see the headline over her picture in the newspaper: "TWELVE-YEAR-OLD SLEUTH SOLVES KIDNAPPING FOR PO-LICE." It was exciting to be able to help someone *and* get some recognition for it.

She got her robe and a towel, not really wanting to swim now, but knowing she ought to. If she stayed here in the apartment for the next hour, she might not be able to resist the refrigerator. And she knew she would only prowl around rest-lessly, not able to settle down to read or even watch TV. She was already nervous at the thought of going over. Her heart seemed to beat faster than normal. It must be that three o'clock was a safe time, because Andy had set the hour so definitely. And, even if it were not, she had to go through with it now.

She got her key and the case for her glasses, slung a towel over her arm, and let herself out the apartment door. She took the elevator down to the second floor, which led out to the pool, did a superficial shower in obedience to the sign at the entrance, and walked out into the blazing sun. The pool was crowded as usual, mostly with little kids who kept pushing each other off the edge of the pool into the shallow end and then screaming with high-pitched laughter.

Vickie watched them tumbling into the water. Some of the children were so little that they were hardly able to walk. She was grateful that Francine had insisted she learn to swim when she was five years old and had gone with her to swimming classes.

"Don't be like I was," Francine had said. "I was always too chicken to try new things. I didn't learn to swim until I was a freshman in high school, and it was embarrassing because all my friends already knew how."

Vickie had never really believed that Francine had been timid and bashful. Now, having seen the picture and having heard what Pete said, she realized there was a lot about Francine that she did not know. Eleven years' difference in their ages sometimes had been a barrier to them. Often, she had just felt like Francine's little sister.

"If Francine can change, so can I," she muttered as she walked over to the diving board.

She plunged in. The water was cold in contrast to the hot rays of the sun. She swam vigorously back and forth across the length, stopping occasionally to peer up at the clock at one end of the pool by the lifeguard's seat. She could read the clock's large face easily, even without her glasses.

Ordinarily she did not bother to check the time, but just swam until she was tired. But today she had to stop in plenty of time to shower and wash and dry her hair and get over to the other apartment. The timing was crucial. Since Andy had set the time, he must know that he would be alone then.

But her long strokes back and forth across the pool seemed to bring other questions, questions she had brushed off before. If Andy could let her into the apartment at a precise time, why could he not just come out by himself? He obviously was not tied down on a chair or a bed. Even his hands would not be tied if he were able to open the door and let her in.

She argued back with herself, trying to answer objections that flooded her mind. Maybe he was not going to open the door. Maybe all he could do was give her information through the door and ask her to call the police. But if so, why hadn't he put the information on his signs. Or why hadn't he given her information when she was over the other time? She hoped she would not have to call the police. Her other tip had not been believed.

The questions came so thick and fast, and were so unanswerable, that she could not concentrate on improving her swimming form and speed. So she hoisted herself, shivering in spite of the hot sun, on to the edge of the pool. The chilled feeling was both from the cold water and from the mystery, which seemed to be harder to figure out the closer she came to solving it.

She peered up at the pool clock again and could

hardly believe that it was only a quarter after two. Time really dragged when you were waiting for something to happen. Before going up to dress, she decided to sit in the sun for a few minutes and dry off. She pulled a deck chair around to let her see the clock and not face the sun, and stretched out near a bunch of little kids who were splashing in the baby pool.

A cluster of young mothers near her were all talking at once. Vickie leaned back against the chair, her eyes closed, not paying any attention to them. Suddenly a snatch of words made her go rigid, and she turned her head to listen.

"Thank goodness, this one is finally settled. The trouble is you never know when it will happen again. When you have little children, you never can be sure they are safe."

"It's terrible!" The mother in the brief green suit reached out to hug the baby sitting beside her in his stroller. "My children are young enough that they are home all day. But I'm already worrying about them when they are old enough to go to school."

Another mother nodded. "People tell us we are crazy to live in the city with small children. But this little boy lived in an expensive suburb, and the place didn't protect him."

"Well, I'm glad he wasn't hurt. Though I imagine he was scared to death the whole time."

Vickie sat up. "Excuse me. Are you talking about the little boy who was kidnapped?"

"Yes. The police found him. Isn't that wonderful?"

"How did you know?"

116

"A special news bulletin was just on the radio." The mother gestured at the small portable radio on the concrete beside her pool chair.

"How did it happen? How did the police find him so fast? I just saw his—" Vickie stopped abruptly.

Better not say anything to them about signs and messages for help.

One of the mothers answered, "I guess the police have been following all the tips that came in, even though some of them sounded impossible. They didn't say much publicly because they didn't want to tip the kidnappers that they were on to them."

So they did believe me.

The thought brought a feeling of relief but also of disappointment. She had been so close to solving the mystery herself that she could not help feeling a twinge of regret that the solution had been snatched from her at the last minute.

She reached for her robe. Maybe she should get dressed and go over to the other building anyway to see what information she could get from the doorman. The worst disappointment was not getting to meet Andy after all the messages they had exchanged.

Then she heard one of the mothers say, "I can just imagine how *my* six-year-old would have felt if he had been tied up for five days in that big old empty warehouse."

"It must have been awful at night," another one replied, shuddering. "Probably there were rats and other things running all over the place."

"An old warehouse?" Vickie echoed. "Is that where they found him—in an old warehouse?"

"Yes. It was an old building that had not been in use for years. The city should have torn it down long ago. I hope it will be now."

"But—but that's impossible!" Vickie exclaimed. "That he was found there, I mean. At least, that's not where he has been all this—"

She stopped abruptly again, aware of their curious stares at her. One of the mothers asked, "Do you know the family?"

Vickie shook her head as she thrust her feet into her thongs and stood up, pulling her robe on wrong side out. Everything seemed upside down. How *could* Andy be on the other side of the city in an old warehouse when she had talked with him by signs an hour ago in an expensive apartment on Linden Boulevard? It did not make sense.

She leaned to grab up her towel as the mother in the green suit asked, "Is something wrong?"

"No—no. I—just—have to do something."

She hurried along the side of the pool, her thongs clip-clopping and sliding on the wet cement. She ducked around the screaming kids, knowing that the bunch of mothers was staring after her. She waited impatiently for the elevator, pushing the button repeatedly even though she knew that that never brought it any faster. When she finally got up to the apartment and tried to put the key into the lock, her hand shook and she could not get the key to turn.

Finally she got the door open and rushed down the hall and through the kitchen to the dining room window. Her eyes immediately found the mysterious window.

The white window shades were in an even, unbroken line. No message pleading for help was plastered against the glass. There was no evidence that anything unusual had happened, nothing to show that the police had been there. She stared down into the courtyard. Surely if the police had come searching, people would still be standing around watching and talking. The only people in the hot sun in the courtyard were a maintenance man trimming the circles of grass and a little girl riding a tricycle slowly around and around the fountain. The quiet, ordinary scene seemed unreal in contrast to the crime that had taken place over there.

Or—she turned away from the window—or the crime she *thought* had taken place over there. She searched for answers. Maybe the kidnappers had moved Andy in this past hour.

Or maybe the report had been wrong. Maybe the police had given out wrong information on purpose to trick the kidnappers into thinking they were safe, and then the police would pounce unexpectedly and rescue Andy.

It was just a little past two-thirty, not the usual time for news, but Vickie flipped on the television anyway. The reporter sitting at his desk, his voice both serious and happy, was just finishing a report.

"So, one frightened little six-year-old is home with his parents after going through a five-day ordeal tied up in an abandoned building at nine-

119

teenth and Broadway. The kidnappers, two men and a woman, are in custody. We will have more details on our six o'clock report. For those of you who have just tuned in, let me repeat. Little Andy has been found. He is safe at home with his parents after having been kept in this old warehouse."

Vickie watched the picture fade from the newsroom and focus on a huge, sprawling building. A dozen or more police cars, lights flashing, still surrounded it. Crowds of people milled around in front of the building and reporters and photographers rushed in from all angles. The rescue must have just happened. She wondered if Francine had been in on it.

Vickie flipped off the television set, feeling a mixture of relief that Andy was safe, but regret that she had not been the one to find him. So much for the headlines she had imagined. It was certainly a good thing she had kept her mouth shut and had not said anything about the signals and messages in the window.

She sighed and turned toward her bedroom to dress. There went her great mystery and her attempt to play detective.

Then she stopped, frowning. The signals and messages! If Andy had not been over there the past few days, then who had been sending the messages? OK, she had been wrong to jump to the conclusion that it was Andy. But she had not imagined the signals. She had seen them. They were real. Someone over there needed help.

Vickie whirled around and hurried to the window. She had been there only a few seconds when one of the white window shades whipped clear to the top of the window and a large poster appeared. Each letter on it was a different color, each one printed very large.

DON'T FORGET
THREE O'CLOCK

She was right. There was a mystery over there. It was not Andy, but it was someone. And this time it was someone only she knew about.

"I'm going over and knock on the door and get into that apartment." She said the words out loud, her voice firm in the empty room.

9

Vickie had been in her swim suit so long that it was dry. So was her hair. But when she started to peel off the suit and get dressed, she remembered her resolution to improve her appearance. That meant showering and washing her hair. If she zipped in and out the way Mom did, and then used Francine's hair dryer, she could be ready in ten minutes. That would leave her five minutes to get down this building and up into the other. She would just make it if the doorman over there would remember her and let her up.

When she dropped the soap in the shower stall three times, got shampoo in her eyes, and then could not get the dryer cord untangled and plugged in quickly, she realized how jittery she was.

The main reason for the nervousness was that the situation facing her now was completely unknown. The other one had been unknown, too, but in a different way. All this time she had been expecting to go over and rescue a kidnapped child. But now she had no idea who was behind that closed door, or who would open it when she knocked.

Her arms felt cold and she rubbed them and wondered, *Should I go over by myself?*

She answered her own question. "I have to. I've promised."

This time she would definitely let Charlie know which apartment she was going to. Probably she should say something to Mac, too, sort of casually, "I'm going over to apartment 1492B."

That way, if anything happened and she did not come back, and her folks tried to trace her movements, Mac would surely remember and tell them where she had gone.

"I might get yanked into the apartment and held prisoner."

She found herself talking out loud with nervousness, and the fluttery feeling in her stomach did not stop, even when she told herself sternly, "Stop being silly!"

When she had zipped into shorts and a shirt, she went to the kitchen and poured herself a glass of milk, closing her eyes and mind to the tempting cookie jar full of chocolate chip oatmeal cookies.

The clock over the refrigerator said eight minutes to three, which gave her time for one last look out the window. She had barely got to the window, not really expecting any more messages, when the shade in the other apartment jerked up and down three times in a violent motion. The movement was uncanny because Vickie could not see anyone at all. It looked as though the shade were jerking all by itself.

Then another sign appeared, the words clearly done in large, heavy, almost angry-looking strokes. The message was unmistakeable.

COME ALONE

Vickie swallowed, feeling more frightened than she had before. Her cold, sweaty hands felt slippery as she gripped the marble window sill. Whoever was over there had been watching for her, hoping she would come to the window, and had had his last desperate message ready. It was as though the prisoner could follow her every move, read her every thought, and was now warning her. She could do only one thing, and that was to obey.

But she also must reassure the person that she would follow instructions. She hurried to the bedroom for the OK sign that she had shoved under the bed and took it back to the window. She counted slowly to herself, "one and two and three and," until she got to thirty. Dad had said once that by counting that way you could estimate time. A half minute should give the person long enough to see her reassurance.

Then she watched the window shade jerk up and down three times in answer. Vickie stuck the sign out of sight under the bed, took her key, and opened the door. She stood irresolute in the open doorway, hating to leave the safety of the apartment. She had a half-formed thought of leaving a note for her mother. Then she shook it away. Mother would not be home for another hour. Surely she would be back by then.

Down deep she knew she still had a faint, lingering doubt that a mystery really existed over there. She had been proved wrong about Andy. If she left a note for her mother and then this proved to be nothing at all, her mother would say in a half-exasperated tone, "Vickie, that imagination of yours! Some day it will get you into real trouble."

She closed the door firmly, and let her feet

carry her quickly along the hall to the elevator. As she waited for it and then stepped into its emptiness, she thought back over all the signals and signs.

First, on Monday, she had noticed the crooked window shade and the white paper with lines of some kind on it. That evening the lights had flashed. Next the SOS sign had appeared and after that the word HELP. Right after that she had gone over to the apartment and had heard the SOS signal tapped from inside. Yesterday she had seen the PLEASE HURRY plea.

Then just a few hours ago had come the request, COME AT THREE and, finally, COME ALONE. She had not imagined any of this. A mystery waited her in that innocent-looking apartment. The final COME ALONE meant that she could not confide even a hint of her mission to either of the doormen. It was all up to her.

She waved nonchalantly at Mac as she crossed the lobby, her rope sandals with the soft soles noiseless on the tile, and pushed through the revolving doors. Now if Charlie only would cooperate and let her up, she would be exactly on time. Could she get by him again by making him think she knew what she was doing?

She remembered Francine once telling them what she had learned about how to get an interview with someone who did not want to talk about himself.

"You have to be very sincerely interested in that person," Francine had explained. "And that's hard because maybe at first you have to fake it some. Being interested and liking the person,

I mean. But then you remember that he or she is a person like you. So you talk on a one-to-one basis as though it's just the two of you sharing things with each other. You take for granted the person wants others to know about him and what concerns him. If you really like people, interviews aren't hard."

Francine had finished with that quick, bright smile that lighted her eyes with warm friendliness—the smile Vickie envied and wished she had.

But I do, she thought now, suddenly in surprise. *I do have it. Or anyway, I can learn to have it. Francine didn't know how to do all this when she was my age. She had to learn how to be friendly. Pete said he had to learn how to make friends fast. I'll have to learn that when school starts—but I can.*

The thought gave her confidence and even made the thought of school seem less hopeless. With quick steps she crossed the tree-lined, circular walks between the two buildings. But even the surge of confidence and the feel of the hot sun on her head were not enough to erase the cold, shaky emptiness inside her. The coolness of the lobby matched the chill in the pit of her stomach as she crossed past the round glass greenhouse with its masses of roses.

"Hi." She smiled at Charlie and walked confidently toward the locked lobby entrance behind which was the bank of elevators.

He moved swiftly but in an unhurried way to block her and said, "Hello, yourself, young lady. Which apartment do you want?"

Before Vickie could answer, his face broke into

126

a welcoming smile, and he said, "Oh, it's you. You were here day before yesterday looking for your friend."

"How can you remember me with all the people you see every day?"

Down deep she was glad he had recognized her. In case she was held in that apartment upstairs, he might remember that she had gone up and not come down.

He shrugged, looking pleased at her surprise. "That's just part of my job. To remember people, I mean."

He moved back behind his desk to be near the telephone, sat down on his high stool, and leaned his elbows on the top of the desk. He was obviously settled for a long talk.

"You see, this job is a very important position. You might say it's a little like being a detective. I'm not here just to open the door for people to go in and out. Anybody could do that." His voice was scornful of such an idea and he shook his head.

Then he went on. "I'm a very important part of the security of this building. I have to train myself to remember people. What they look like, what time they leave in the morning, what time they return. I even have to remember who goes in and out with the regular tenants. That's not easy, because I have to remember little things about them. How they dress, how they walk, whether they say thank you when you help them or just expect you to help. Yes sir, everybody is different. And I have to remember all that."

Vickie tried to look interested. But it was already two minutes before three and she still had to get through the locked door and up in the elevator to floor fourteen. She edged toward the door, but he stayed behind his desk, not seeming to notice her at all as he went on reminiscing about how he had stopped people whom he had suspected of wanting to visit friends unannounced.

If he only knew what I have planned, he would be upset, Vickie thought. *Maybe he wouldn't brag so much on himself if he knew a person my age had already gotten past him once.*

It was kind of a scary thought though, because if she could do it, maybe other people could, too. Her idea of kidnappers getting past the doorman was not so way out after all.

Just as she began to despair of getting past him, two elderly ladies came in from shopping and he hurried to unlock the door and hold it open for them. Vickie slipped in behind them, watched as they rang for the elevator, and listened to Charlie's explanation.

"I've just given you an example of my good detective work. Did you notice that I didn't question those ladies about who they were or what apartment they wanted? Now, it wasn't just because they were carrying groceries," he added, shaking his head. "A new man who didn't have any experience might have just supposed they belonged here because they were each carrying a paper bag of groceries. But *I* know better. You see, that could be just a dodge a crook used to get in. Know what I mean? Someone just pretending to live here by carrying in sacks of groceries. I don't mean those two little ladies might be crooks," he added hastily. "I recognized them. Just like I recognized you when I'd only seen you once. I remembered you came the other day to visit your friend."

He looked at her proudly, waiting for her answer.

Vickie nodded. "You *are* good. I'm interested in detective work, too. Maybe you can give me some more pointers another time."

She backed away, moved toward the elevators, and pressed the up button. She smiled back at him, but inside she was churning with impatience. As he nodded at her, he touched his hand to his cap in a salute. Then he turned to his desk to answer the phone.

Vickie was glad after all that she had not told him what apartment she was going to. Not that she had had a chance to say anything. What a talker! But at least he had been so busy bragging on himself that he had not really checked her out.

She stood nervously waiting for the elevator, hoping no one else would get on when she did. What would she do if someone else got off at the fourteenth floor and asked who she was? When the elevator came, she got on quickly, pressed the ivory knob, and stood still as it rose quickly and silently to floor fourteen.

When it stopped and the doors slid open, she felt as though her feet were glued to the floor. She had to force herself to hold the doors open and look out into the softly lighted hall. Again she thought how quiet apartment buildings were in the daytime. The silence had a waiting, watchful quality, as though it sensed danger. She resisted

129

the impulse to press the down knob, which would let the elevator hurtle her down to safety. She had promised to come.

She licked her dry lips and swallowed to make her throat less dry as she stepped out into the hall and heard the elevator doors slide shut behind her. Moving slowly, she walked silently along the carpeted floor and turned the corner to go to the apartment at the far end of the hall.

Suddenly she froze as some sixth sense made her certain that she was not alone on the floor. Something else was there, a presence she could feel rather than see. She had often read about people being so scared that their hair stood on end. She was sure her hair must be sticking straight up now as she waited for someone to grab her suddenly from behind. Perhaps this was what the whole mystery was about—someone trying to get her over to the building. Someone deliberately trying to harm her for no sane reason.

She stood frozen in the middle of the hall, her breath caught in her throat in a soundless scream. Her hands were clenched so tightly that she could feel her fingernails digging into her palms. A flicker of movement just beyond her range of vision held her motionless.

She slowly turned her head. Then her shoulders collapsed. Feeling weak and shaken with relief she leaned against the wall. A cat sat in front of the apartment door on the other side of the hall. Its thick tail was curled around its sleek gray coat and its green eyes stared at her from a broad white face.

The management in their building had a strict

rule of no pets except for goldfish. This building probably did too.

"I ought to turn your owners in for letting you roam the hall and scare me to death," she whispered at it.

The cat ignored her, yawned widely, and then stared at her, its green eyes unblinking.

Vickie hurried her steps along the hall. Her watch said eight minutes after three. As she passed the stairway with the red "Stairs" sign, she reached out to open the door quietly. She stepped into the little hall with the landing, where she had stood once before, and looked down over the railing. It would be a long way down to the ground floor, but if she had to she could duck into here and run down the stairs. It would be faster—and safer—than waiting for the elevator. Everything hinged on what waited for her behind that closed apartment door.

She stepped back into the hall, leaving the exit door standing partway open. Now she was right outside the door with the large 1492B lettered on the outside. The narrow, gold-plated slot on the door was empty. Most people slipped in a name card. The name card on their door was fancy, each letter ornately swirled by her mother.

Their safe apartment seemed remote as she stood waiting, acutely aware of how scared she was of whatever lay on the other side of the door. Her hands felt clammy again and she wiped them down her shorts and then rubbed them together to warm them.

She put her ear against the door but could not hear any sound from inside. She raised her hand to knock, and then stopped. How would the person in there know that it was she and not someone else? He—or she—might have given up on her, especially since she was late. They should have arranged some kind of signal.

The thought triggered an idea. Of course they had a signal, one they had already used, even though then she thought it was Andy using it. She reached and tapped it out, saying the words silently.

dot-dot-dot, dash-dash-dash, dot-dot-dot

She listened, but no answer came back. *Was* she too late after all? *Had* she failed someone in need by not being on time? She tried turning the doorknob slowly and pushing the door. It was locked as she was sure it would be.

Just as she raised her hand to knock again, this time loudly and without the SOS, someone yanked the door open.

10

Vickie stared down at the figure before her. In her wildest imagining of how the person sending such desperate messages for help would look, she had never expected what appeared so suddenly before her. She stared, open-mouthed, at the girl who was leaning against the cushioned back of a wheelchair.

She was thin, with one leg in a cast and her neck supported by a high, wide collar. Vickie remembered that her mother had worn one like that for several months a couple of years ago when she had a whiplash from a minor car accident. Through the girl's thin cotton blouse Vickie could see that a cast covered her body from just under her arms down to her hips.

But when she looked at the girl's face under a mass of curly blond hair, she saw the dancing lights in the girl's blue eyes and the impish grin as she laughed up into Vickie's startled expression.

She reached with her narrow white hands to back the chair away from Vickie, who stood in the open door, and invited, "Come in. I had begun to think I was never going to get you over here."

Vickie stepped hesitantly inside, heard the door whoosh shut behind her and the automatic lock click, and reached too late to grab the doorknob.

One thing she had decided before she came was not to get trapped in the apartment. And now she was.

But as she stood by the closed door and looked around, the familiarity of the place made her relax. The wide hall, so much like theirs, was flooded with sunshine pouring in from windows in the adjoining rooms. The sun reflected on the hall chandeliers, making them glitter. A long glass etageré against one wall was filled with a collection of silver and crystal dishes. The sun sparkled off them in gold and blue flashes of light. Flowering plants along the opposite wall also were bathed in sunlight and were a mass of green and orange and yellow flowers.

The color contrast to the varied, muted silver and blue shades of the decorating scheme in their apartment was startling, and made everything here seem alive and glowing. How ridiculous to think that anything unpleasant or dangerous could happen in such vivid surroundings.

Vickie unhesitatingly followed the girl as she wheeled the chair around and maneuvered it through the hall and into the sunny living room.

Neither of them had spoken since the girl's invitation. Now she turned her chair to face Vickie and again laughed up at her.

"I'm glad finally to see you face to face instead of through a window across the courtyard—two windows really, yours and mine."

"But then you aren't—"

Vickie stopped, bewildered. She had meant to say, "You aren't a prisoner here? You aren't a kidnap victim?"

134

She realized how silly it would sound to say that in this glowing room to the girl with laughter in her eyes. So she finished the sentence, "I mean, are you all alone?"

The girl laughed again at the confused sound in Vickie's voice and answered, "Yep. Everybody goes places these days but me."

Vickie stared down at the leg cast, then at the body cast, and quickly looked away. Long ago her folks had taught her not to stare at anyone who was different, no matter what the reason. But it was hard not to now as the girls stood facing each other.

But the girl seemed not to notice Vickie's embarrassment. "Come on. Let me show you where I sat to watch you."

Vickie followed the wheelchair across the living room and into the dining room, feeling as though she were walking through her own apartment. The girl gestured out the window.

"I could see you standing over there, and sitting at your table eating. That made me sure your layout was just like ours. I knew you must have moved in while I was still in the hospital because I hadn't seen you before. When I saw you last Monday, and thought you must be about my age, I was *so* glad."

Vickie looked out the window and down the two floors to their eleventh floor. She easily picked out their apartment and could see the baskets of fern in the dining room window. But she could not see into the room. She turned, puzzled. "How could you see *me* so plainly?"

"With my binoculars," the girl answered matter-of-factly. "I could see everything you did when you were sitting at the table. I could even see the milk in your glass and almost tell the color of jam on your toast and what brand of cereal you were eating."

Vickie felt uncomfortable. That's what Dad had meant when he warned against her using the binoculars to see what people were doing. She did feel spied on. Her privacy had been invaded.

But all she said in answer was, "How come I couldn't see you?" She did not add, "Even the time I used binoculars," because she did not want to admit that she had used them a couple of times. She especially avoided saying that because she was never going to use them again, except outside in the park.

"Probably because I'm half lying down, and because we are a couple of floors higher than you. If we were lower, you would have seen me because you'd be looking down on me the way I was on you."

She laughed up at Vickie again and said, "The only thing I couldn't tell about you was your name. I'm Diane. Diane Stewart."

"And I'm Vickie Montgomery."

Then Vickie burst out, "But what about all the SOS signals? And the mysterious notes in the window?"

"Well, I had to do something to get your attention, didn't I?" Diane demanded. "I wanted to find out who you were."

"Sure, but you could have just called information and gotten my phone number—"

"I didn't know your name," Diane interrupted.

"Or what your apartment number was. Of course, I could have figured that out easy enough. You figured out mine."

"Well, why didn't you just wave at me or something?"

Diane's smile flashed again. "That's too ordinary," she protested. "I thought it would be more fun to make a mystery out of it. Since I didn't know anything about you, I didn't know if we would hit it off or not. Sure I could have found your phone number and called you. Or gone over and asked your doorman about you. But I wanted to be sure we thought alike. See, I thought you probably always ate at the same place when you were alone and naturally that meant you would be looking out in my direction. I figured that if you would notice a window shade that was crooked when it never had been before, then I'd know we would be compatible."

Vickie looked at her. Compatible. That word she knew. Dad had said once that people did not have to be exactly alike to be good friends. But if they had similar ideas and interests, then they would be compatible.

"Was that morning, last Monday, the first time the shade was crooked?"

Diane nodded. "I had just come home from the hospital on Saturday. I was trying to figure out how to make the days go by faster. My mother works and is gone all day so there's not even anyone to talk to. And she hadn't had time to get to the library to stock me up on books. I got a bunch of new ones when I went to the hospital, but I'd read 'em all a couple of hundred times."

She looked up at Vickie and demanded, "Do you like to read? I hope?"

When Vickie nodded, she asked, "What's your favorite?"

Without waiting for an answer, she wheeled her chair around and said, "Come on to my room. My favorites are mysteries. Any kind. Look, I've got practically all of Nancy Drew and lots of Phyllis Whitney stories. I even like Sherlock Holmes except that he does an awful lot of talking."

Vickie stared around the room, which seemed all bookshelves with books spilled out on the floor and stacked up beside the bed.

"My mother said if I didn't like to read, I'd have driven her out of her mind trying to figure out things for me to do while I'm stuck in this wheelchair."

She stopped to grin impishly at Vickie. "I can tell you're dying to know what's wrong with me and you won't ask because your mother told you it isn't polite to ask questions of people in wheelchairs. Right?"

Vickie nodded, smiling back. Diane was going to be fun to know.

"OK, so I'm asking. What's wrong with you?"

"I've got scoliosis."

"Sco—?"

"—li-o-sis. Scoliosis."

"What's that?"

"Don't worry. It's nothing catching. And the word makes it sound worse than it really is—I guess. It means my spine is twisted to one side."

She looked up and caught the unspoken ques-

138

tion in Vickie's eyes and said hastily, "Oh, I don't mean I can't walk. The wheelchair bit is just my mother's idea."

"How long have you had this sco— whatever it is?"

Diane's voice had a touch of impatience as she said, "Look, the word isn't that hard to say if you do it slowly. It's sco-li-o-sis."

Then she shrugged and answered Vickie's question. "I've had it a long time, I guess. It sort of happened gradually. My mother used to yell at me all the time because she thought I wasn't standing up straight. You know, the 'You'll be sorry later on' routine. Then I was in a car accident last month. I broke my leg and hurt my neck. When I was in the hospital for that, my mother told the doctor about my walking crooked, and he did some tests and found out that my spine is crooked."

"Can they fix it?"

"Yeah. First I had to have an operation, so I guess it was a good thing I had the accident and was already in the hospital. I have to wear a plaster cast, which is what this is," she explained, pulling her blouse up to show it. "I wear this for three months and then a plastic cast for about four months. The reason for the cast is that they put a steel rod down beside my spine to straighten it. That will be there forever, I guess."

"Can you go to school with the cast on?"

"Oh, sure. I won't be able to take gym or do any of the fun stuff for a couple of years, but otherwise I can do everything. The wheelchair isn't because of the scoliosis. I'm using it only until my leg cast is off. My mother didn't want me running around during the day while she was gone—in case I tripped and fell. So she got me the chair and made me promise to stay in it when she wasn't here."

The more Diane rattled on, spilling out words, the more certain Vickie was that they were going to hit it off super.

"How long have you lived here?"

"Just since the end of May," Diane answered. "We moved here from Colorado because my mother wanted to get away from everybody she knew. Too many bad memories out there. And she knew somebody here who got her a really neat job. My dad split awhile back. About Christmas. He pays a lot of alimony, so my mother wouldn't have to work, but she likes to. She'd go nuts if she had to stay home all day with nothing to do but polish furniture."

Diane tossed out the information in such an offhand way that it took Vickie a couple of minutes to realize what she had said about her father. That must mean her parents were divorced. Diane sounded as though not having her father around did not bother her a bit.

Vickie had a funny feeling in her stomach. What would it be like if Dad were not home? What if he just walked off and did not care how she and Francine and Mom were getting along? Nothing would go right for them. They needed him.

She was snatched back to listening again as Diane said, "Now tell me all about you. First, what grade are you in?"

"Seventh. Going into it."

Diane gave a long, satisfied sigh. "I hoped you were. I am too. We're the only two people in the apartments who are school age, I think, unless all the others are away on vacation. I've only seen little kids playing outside. I really hated to think of going to a new school all alone."

"Me too," Vickie answered fervently.

"Once in a while I felt like throwing open a window and yelling out, 'Hey, somebody, help me! I need a friend!'" She stopped and grinned. "Of course it was a dumb idea since no one would answer."

Call unto Me, and I will answer you. The words on the back of Dad's business card pushed their way into Vickie's mind. She almost said the words out loud, but caught herself in time. She did not want Diane to laugh at her when they had just met. Anyway, Dad was the one to ask about the words' real meaning. He was finding great and wonderful things in the Bible. And maybe—was it possible there was a God who knew about her, who knew how much she needed a friend? Had He answered and sent Diane? It was a frightening thought but a comforting one, too.

Looking at Diane's happy face, she felt a big load slide from her mind. Going to school all alone, the thing she had dreaded most and had not even been able to put into words to her family, was not a worry anymore. She had a friend.

She wondered if she should risk telling Diane all she had imagined about the kidnapping. She decided to try, even at the risk of Diane's thinking she was kind of dumb.

She took a deep breath and smiled across the sunny room. "You said you liked mysteries. I do, too. In fact, I had a really neat one all worked out. One that was happening right in this apartment."

Diane's eyes sparkled. "What kind? And why this apartment?" She stopped, looked across at Vickie, and then burst out, "Because of my signs, I'll bet! What kind of mystery did you think it was?"

"Did you hear about the little boy who was kidnapped?"

"Yeah. He was found just today. But what does that have to do with my signs?" She stopped and then plunged on, "You mean—you—you thought he was here? That he was the one signalling you?"

Vickie nodded, and then let her breath out in a sigh of relief as Diane exclaimed eagerly, "Sure, I can see how you would."

"You see, I couldn't see anyone over here. I'd heard a lot about the kidnapping because my sister is a TV news reporter—"

"She is? How neat!"

"Well, she's really just starting," Vickie hurried to explain. "I mean, she's not a big star with her own show or anything. But anyway, when the SOS sign came and then the word HELP, naturally I thought right away about the little boy."

"Sure, I would have too," Diane agreed again. "And when you came over and tapped the SOS rhythm on the door, and I answered—"

"Then I was sure I was right," Vickie broke in.

142

She stopped and looked at Diane. "Why didn't you let me in that time?"

"I'm sorry. I just thought it would be more fun to carry the signals on a little longer. It was a lot of fun to see you come to the window and look to see if I had another sign in my window. If I'd known you were really' worried about what was going on over here, I would have opened the door."

"That did make it more exciting," Vickie admitted. "But of course it made me more sure than ever that Andy was here. I thought he was tied up and couldn't let me in. And your messages kept coming. When I heard he was found, but not here, I didn't know what to think. I was just glad I hadn't told anyone my suspicions. Not even my parents."

"Yeah, and I put my last sign in the window today after they found him!" Diane's voice was high-pitched with excitement. "What did you think when you saw it?"

"I was really glad to know there was still a mystery over here," Vickie admitted. "I was feeling disappointed that Andy had been found, which was awful, and really I wasn't sorry. But I'd been so sure I was going to be the big heroine and do something the police couldn't do. When it fizzled, I was kind of down. Then when I saw your sign, I was sure I was on to an even bigger mystery."

"I'll bet you were scared to come over," Diane said, and Vickie heard the admiring note in her voice. "I would have been. But if I'd been in your place I couldn't have stayed away either.

143

We're probably alike in lots of ways, so I know we're going to be friends. I'm so glad you moved here."

"I'm glad too."

Vickie smiled back at Diane and knew she was being absolutely truthful.

Moody Press, a ministry of the Moody Bible Institute, is designed for education, evangelization, and edification. If we may assist you in knowing more about Christ and the Christian life, please write us without obligation: Moody Press, c/o MLM, Chicago, Illinois 60610.